THE END OF TIME
MURDER ON THE MISSISSIPPI

First Published in Great Britain 2016 by Mirador Publishing

First edition: 2016

Any reference to real names and places are purely fictional and are constructs of the author. Any offence the references produce is unintentional and in no way reflects the reality of any locations or people involved.

A copy of this work is available through the British Library.

ISBN: 978-1-911044-48-2

Mirador Publishing
Mirador
Wearne Lane
Langport
Somerset
TA10 9HB

THE END OF TIME
Murder on the Mississippi

By Tom and Sharon Savage
Illustrated by Sharon Savage

Table of Contents

Cast of Characters

Job W. Rankin (J.W.): Funeral parlor director in Muscatine
Minnie Rankin: Job Rankin's wife
Chief Bronner: Chief of Police of Muscatine
R.S. McNutt: Mayor of Muscatine
Dr. Fulliam: Physician
D.W. Truxell: Personal friend of George Volger
Fitch Swan: Jeweler, murderer
Mollie Swan: Fitch Swan's deceased wife
Elsie (Corey) Swan: Fitch Swan's wife
George Volger: Jeweler, athlete, Manager of Muskies basketball team,
          victim
Helen Volger: Wife of George Volger the jeweler
Harriet Cadle: Fitch Swan's sister, mother of Cornelius Cadle
Cornelius Cadle: Fitch Swan's nephew, son of Harriet, Fitch's sister, jeweler
Anna Fraleigh: Aunt of Elsie Swan who raised Elsie
Emma Braunwarth: One of first female physicians in Iowa
Sarah Braunwarth: One of first female physicians in Iowa
Carrie Nation: Women's temperance leader
A.C. Rankin: Ms. Nation's manager
George Volger: Saloon owner, father of George Volger the jeweler
Adam Von Dresky: Saloon owner
L.C. Lang: Proprietor of German Village
Crippen: Proprietor of The Well
George Volger III: Jeweler George Volger's son
William Underdonk: Reporter of Lilly Dry Goods Store fire
David Porter: Elsie's former supervisor at Lilly Dry Goods Store
Chief Brown: Head of Muscatine's first professional fire department
Charles Burroughs: Charged with taking sod from Weed Park

Zimmerman: German Foreign Minister who telegraphed diplomats in Mexico and Japan prior to US entry into WWI

President Woodrow Wilson: United States President from 1913 to 1921

Connie: Helen and George Volger's neighbor

Reverend John Haefner: Pastor of Zion Lutheran Church

Dr. Oliver: Inciter of crowd and filer of charges against Rev. Haefner

Joel McGary: Swan's auctioneer

Floyd Crow & J.H. Walter: Filed charges against Joel McGary

Mrs. Philip Snowden: Suffragette from England

President William Howard Taft: United States President from 1909 to 1913

Carrie Chapman Catt: Leader in women's suffrage movement; Formed League of Women Voters

Newton Quinn: Man hired to be manager of planned Volger Jewelry Store in Davenport

L.A. Willets: Davenport Optometrist who planned to open in the Volger Davenport Jewelry Store

Julius Hayden: Salesman who visited Swan and Volger stores day before murder

Miss Sarah Bilkey: Lived over the Swan Jewelry Store

Mrs. Milan P. Harlow: Elsie Swan's sister of Hartford, Connecticut

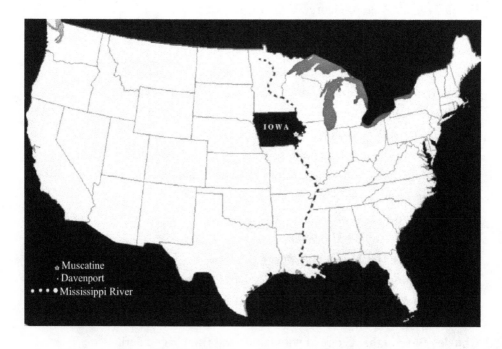

☆ Muscatine
· Davenport
●●●●Mississippi River

Second Street 1913

The End of Time

Come meet me at my water's edge
beneath the silent moon
where ripples touch against the shore
with secrets yet to come.

Prologue

The Mississippi River rests within an ancient crack in the face of the earth. Ten thousand years ago ice sheets melted, crumbled and forced a small section of the river's course to be altered to a new direction. It was upon this unique and diverse course that the small town of Muscatine, Iowa was built.

The constant pulse of the Mississippi beats within the essence of this land and its people.

It echoes the significance of what began in that ancient fissure and resonates throughout history. It begins with the flicker of the tadpole beneath its murky waters and endures with the eagles soaring overhead. It is found in the steam rising over the frozen landscapes in the winter and the life nestled warmly within its feet of chocolate silt.

Chapter 1

Sunday, July 31st of 1921 began as a normal day for Job W. Rankin. *An early morning call on Sunday,* he thought. *In small town Iowa, there is no such thing as a day off for people who deal with the public, especially people in my business. I guess it's asking too much for folks to refrain from dying on Sunday.*

Gnats swarmed around his head while he hurried along Second Street at noon. Sweat beaded his brow and dampened his shirt as he returned to his undertaking parlor, from an early morning call. The summer heat and humidity had been hard to tolerate and was particularly fierce at noontime. It was made worse by the fact that J.W. felt he had to wear appropriate undertaker attire at all times. "It just wouldn't show proper respect for the dearly departed or their loved ones to be walking around in short sleeves," he often said. "There is a certain price a person has to pay to have the responsibility of community undertaker."

J.W. had thought it best to locate his funeral parlor in the downtown area built upon the Mississippi River. The fathers of the community expanded from the river to transport the timber from their lumber industries and to facilitate the many needs of the clam industry from which Muscatine derived pearl buttons. This area continued to be the locus of contact for the retail population, and for his customers.

In addition to being the core of the business district, the area was also a hub for river insects which manifested in the constant drone of aggressive mosquitoes and river gnats. May flies had become so thick this spring that J.W. could hardly breathe. Their dead bodies formed a slimy and slippery coating on all surfaces. Although it was already July, they were still hanging on. *I can handle this. I can deal with this,* J.W. thought. *I see so much of death every day that I need to realize how lucky I am to be alive... in spite of the heat and the bugs. However, I do think I will call it a day after I drop off some papers in the funeral parlor.*

What he wanted to do most was to sit on the front porch with his wife, Minnie and drink some home-made lemonade. Sundays with Minnie had become precious to J.W. At times he would take off his jacket and shoes and maybe even his shirt and lay on his front porch swing while Minnie read to him. At other times he sipped lemonade or limeade as he listened to the many songbirds warbling in the background. Those were his favorite times. Death and dying would be pushed to the back of his mind and he would find peace in the rhythms of the wildlife that gathered along the Mississippi.

Chapter 2

J.W. opened the unlocked door of the funeral parlor and walked inside the dimly lit room. He had taken several steps into the space and was halfway to the workroom when he noticed something strange out of the corner of his eye. There, on the couch in the front area, lay Fitch Swan, the community's premier jeweler and watchmaker and one of the most highly respected businessmen in the community. He was also a friend and neighbor of J.W.

How odd that he would be laying here at this time of the day. Maybe he has some business to discuss with me and has fallen asleep while waiting. It wouldn't seem that unusual since most everybody was exhausted these days by the July heat.

As he walked across the room he asked, "Hello Fitch, have you been waiting for me?" There was no answer. He asked louder, "Fitch, what can I do for you?" Still no response. "For God's sake, Fitch, wake up. It is the middle of the day!" Nothing but silence.

It was then that he noticed that Fitch didn't look quite right. As he walked toward him, a familiar undertaker instinct came upon J.W. He leaned over the body for a closer inspection and realized with shock and certainty, that Fitch Swan was dead.

Oh my God, Fitch. What has happened to you?

J.W. took a deep breath as he worked to overcome feelings of panic. He noticed a key next to the body with an open note that read, "I have killed George Volger. His body is in the back of the store." (The Muscatine Journal and News Tribune, August 1, 1921, pg 1)

As dizziness overcame him, J.W. sat down next to the body and concentrated on steadying his breathing and calming himself. *Good Lord, what have you done, my friend? What have you done? Why didn't you come to me for help, Fitch?* He then noticed another note near the body that was sealed and addressed to Chief of Police, Bronner. The area around the notes was sprinkled with irregularly shaped small crystals. J.W. knew better than to touch any of these things. The parlor of his establishment had now become a crime scene and his friend and neighbor appeared to have become a criminal. He knew what he needed to do. J.W. went to the phone and called the chief of police.

Chapter 3

"Hello. Chief of Police Bronner here."

"Chief, this is J.W. I am sorry to call you on a Sunday but I need your help."

"What can I do for you, J.W.?"

"Fitch Swan is lying dead in my funeral parlor. I found him just now. I don't know what happened. He was here when I walked in. There is a note saying he killed somebody. There is also a note to you that I have not opened."

The phone was silent for several seconds. "Does it say who he killed? Is there another body in your building?"

"It says that he killed George Volger and that the body is in Fitch's store."

"I'll be right there, J.W. Don't touch or move anything. I will need to make a few calls.

Are you absolutely certain that Fitch is dead?"

"Yes, Chief, I am very familiar with death. He has been gone for a while. It looks like this occurred earlier this morning."

"Just stay there by the phone, J.W. and wait until you hear me drive up. Lock the door and don't let anybody in unless I am present."

Chief Bronner hung up the phone and said to his family that was just finishing lunch,

"Something dreadful has happened. You all go ahead and take the children fishing as we had planned. I will be busy all day. It sounds like we have a couple of corpses on our hands right here in downtown Muscatine."

"Was there an accident or something?" asked his wife.

"It sounds like no accident. It sounds like murder."

"Who? Where?"

"I don't have time to talk about it now. I'm not really sure what has happened. I will fill you in on all details tonight. It will probably be late."

The chief phoned Mayor R. S. McNutt, Dr. Fulliam and D.W. Truxell and asked them to meet him downtown outside of the funeral parlor as soon as they could possibly get there. (The Muscatine Journal and News Tribune, August 1, 1921, pg 1)

He arrived at the establishment shortly before the others to find J.W. waiting for him at the front door. "Thank heaven you are here," said J.W. The chief took several steps inside of the door and instructed Rankin to lock it again. He viewed Fitch's body lying on the couch in the front parlor and read the open note. He then picked up the folded and sealed note that Swan had left for him. He opened it carefully and spent several silent moments scanning its contents then refolded it along the same lines and buttoned it into the inside pocket of his uniform shirt. (The Muscatine Journal and News Tribune, August 1, 1921, pg 1)

Chief Bronner stepped outdoors and briefly informed the mayor, doctor and D.W. Truxell who had gathered, of the chain of events, as he understood them. He said, "Gentlemen, I think that we need to all walk together to Swan's store to see what is there. We must proceed slowly and observe closely so that we can all be witness to what lies within."

With a mixture of dread and anxiety all four men approached the building. Not a word was spoken as the mayor unlocked the front door and led the way into the business establishment. He walked slowly through the front room and then entered the back workroom. There he found George Volger, lying face down in a pool of blood.

The doctor examined the body and found a bullet hole in the back of Mr. Volger's skull. The hole would indicate that the fatal weapon had been a 32-caliber revolver. (The Muscatine Journal and News Tribune, August 1, 1921, pg 6)

It did not take long for word to spread about these tragic circumstances in small town Iowa. "Following the tragedy, news spread throughout the city in a few minutes and to surrounding cities by means of telegrams. Hundreds of people gathered in front of the Swan store where the body of Mr. Volger lay. Police were busy keeping the curiosity seekers from entering the store. No one was admitted save police officers and deputies, the county officers, physicians and newspaper men." (The Muscatine Journal and News Tribune, August 1, 1921, pg 6)

All people present were pondering the question of what had occurred here. The gentlemen involved were well acquainted and had worked together in the jewelry business. What had caused a leading and respected businessman, the proprietor of the longest established commercial enterprise in the community, to murder another jeweler? How could this possibly have taken place in the peaceful and friendly small Midwestern town of Muscatine, Iowa?

Although rumors continue to this day about the peculiar happenings of that July Sunday, history has long erased the certainty of the course of events. The facts that remain are but dusty notations and faded clippings. If these remnants that exist are placed in the kaleidoscope of early 20th century America and viewed through a particular prism, the resulting chain of motivations and events come into focus. Although no certainty exists in the following collection of precious stones, a jeweler's spark of authenticity, of probability, may be detected therein.

Book 1

Come hear me at my water's edge
and listen to the song
of fears forgotten, hopes long past
and time when dreams were young.

The passage of life in this small Iowa community is tied to the ebb and flow of the Mississippi River. It connects Muscatine to the world and has allowed commerce and trade to flourish through the early use of river transport and the more recent placement of railroad tracks along its shoreline. The ribbons of iron have not deadened the pulse of the river, but instead have added to the, at times, discordant cacophony.

There is a certain rhythm, a certain timing to the music of the river. Its ancient song includes steaming ice in the winter, flooding in the spring, turtles crawling up from its slime and fish surfacing for nibbles of the plentiful insects that hover over its summer surface. In recent time the river has reflected the more exacting and precise cadences of the residents that have gathered near its banks. Time was now measured in the sounds of the train that meant early morning or noon and the river boats that announced various daily passages.

The toot of the river boat whistles and the loud blasts of the trains called to Fitch. He was a sensitive man, a caring man, an artistic man and was capable of hearing the river song. Not all residents were able to speak its language.

The sounds of the wildlife began when the first silver rays of sunlight reflected on the river. As the sun rose higher, the chorus became louder and the sounds more varied, until they reached a crescendo at full sunrise.

Fitch Swan

Chapter 1:1907
Fitch Swan

I am awakened by the excited chatter of bird song through my lace curtains. These early sounds are one of the reasons that I enjoy living on the top of a bluff overlooking the Mississippi River. As the morning comes into focus, I recall how Mollie felt that she could understand and interpret the bird calls. She had taught me to listen so carefully that I got to the point where I could hear many different languages and accents in their communications. Try as I might, however, I could not understand their meanings.

These early morning sounds are one of the reasons that I enjoy living in this large red brick home that Mollie and I built on the top of a bluff overlooking the river. Mollie said that it felt like "we were on top of the world". Every morning we listened to the bird song through the fluttering lace. Mollie mused at how the shadows of light shining through the lace curtains, danced to the melodies of the birds.

Now is the time to concentrate on the present. My Mollie is gone and this fine May day is the beginning of a new adventure. Tonight I am going to marry Elsie Corey and this home of Mollie's will become her own. I feel certain that Elsie will also love this home. Anybody in this town would be proud to live at the top of East Hill.

In the period of deep sadness that I experienced following the death of my first wife, Mollie Howe, I often looked to the heavens and asked her why she had left me behind. I begged her to come back to earth and to take me with her. I attempted to communicate with her through the wildlife and especially the birds of the river. It was to no avail. She was gone.

We were young when we married and had so many plans for our future. We intended to have a large family and live in a large house and own a large business. Everything was going to be the biggest and the best for us. We were optimistic about our potential. The fruits of life were ripe and waiting for harvest. We were able to build this comfortable home because my jewelry business was the largest and most successful in the community. Unfortunately we were not able to have a family and to realize all of our dreams before her demise.

****

Today I am not experiencing any anxiety at all as I dress for my marriage to Elsie. I remember my first glimpse of her. I was arranging the display in the window of my jewelry store on Second Street after a shipment of necklaces designed with prime amber stones, had arrived. I noticed that the light golden tones in the amber were similar to the hues in a large carved oak time piece that I had in the store. I fetched the clock and was pleased with the way they complimented each other.

I suddenly got that eerie feeling of being watched. I glanced up from my work and was startled by the sight of a beautiful young lady whose brown curly locks glistened in the sunlight with the same golden amber tone as my window display. Her hair had a most unusual frizzy nature that caused her to appear to have a gilded halo surrounding her head.

"Who is that beautiful gem?" I muttered to myself as I smiled and waved at the girl. Just then she looked directly into my eyes, smiled shyly, turned and walked away. It immediately struck me that her eyes had precisely matched the aquamarine stones that I stocked. "My word," I said. "She truly is a gem."

I was startled as my young employee, George Volger, chuckled behind me. "You certainly have impeccable taste, Mr. Swan. That is Elsie Corey. She works down the street at Lilly's department store. She was a few grades ahead of me when we were in school. Yes she is a gem. I had a crush on her for most of my childhood but I guess she thought I was too young for her." I was annoyed by George's intrusion into my thoughts. I had not meant to speak aloud.

"Thanks for the information, George. Please help me clean up all of this packing material." While I busied myself with the finishing touches on the store window, I tried to contain my amusement. It had been a long time since I have felt any attraction to a woman. I always thought that my standards of beauty were too high and that I would never meet another woman as attractive as my Mollie.

An appreciation of beauty is something I have always possessed. Instead of playing ball like the other young men, I preferred to engage in more artistic

24

endeavors which didn't do much for my popularity. The lunch breaks from my clerking job at the dry-goods store were often spent in the jewelry stores where I would admire the gems and the delicate gold and silver handiwork. I was fascinated by the precision and detail involved in the repair of clocks and watches. It is funny how this tendency which people once saw as a defect, is now viewed as an asset.

One of the jewelers offered me a job as a clerk and jeweler-in-training after observing me in his store several times. I trained in the art of jewelry making for several years and found that it suited my artistic sensibilities. Eventually, I opened my own business in 1876 in the center of the business district on Second Street. I developed my store into "one of the well appointed establishments of the city". I was proud to know that it was said in town that "I carried a large and well selected line of jewelry of both foreign and domestic manufacture" and that it was the "honorable and straightforward business methods which I employed that advanced me far on the high road to success". (History of Muscatine County, Iowa, Irving B. Richman, Supervising Editor. Chicago: S. J. Clarke Publishing Co., 1911. 2 v., pg 89)

My jewelry and watch making business was successful from its beginning and I was soon reaping a considerable profit. I was not raised in a wealthy family and this newly found prosperity provided a feeling of freedom that I had never experienced. I could and did surround myself with valuable objects and filled my life with treasure and affluence. These items of value somehow made me feel as if I, myself, had more significance. Therefore, unfortunately, I found that once I became accustomed to beautiful objects it was increasingly difficult to deny myself the satisfaction of those acquisitions.

The realization came to me that I might have a problem and need to rein in my spending a bit when the safe that I purchased for the store in 1883 arrived. It was described as the "finest safe in Iowa" and was on exhibition for six weeks at the Chicago Exposition. How could I let that opportunity pass? It was 6 feet high, 3 feet deep, 4 feet 3 inches wide and weighed 9000 pounds. Artistic embellishments were on a grand scale. The inner doors displayed a fountain scene with tropical fruits and flowers enlivened with birds of paradise and butterflies. The inside of the outer doors had a woodland scene on one side and a moonlit lake scene on the other. A beautiful expanse of water stretched across both outside front doors, enclosing an island. In the background on the main shore, the slogan "Love is a Cottage" was printed and symbolized by two swans sporting in the lake. The lower parts of the doors were decorated with festoons of roses and other flowers. The two sides of the safe were ornamented with clusters of poppies and peonies in bud and in blossom, and spangle winged moths and butterflies, poised and flying. (Muscatine Daily Journal, November 6, 1883, pg 2)

Sweat dripped and muscles groaned as I assisted the workmen in lugging the safe up the rickety back steps and into my rather small store. The movers all began to giggle at the sight of the highly decorated structure in its location in the cramped and dimly lit back room.

"Well maybe it is a bit too much," I mused.

"It looks like it belongs in a castle," said one of the men. "King George would love it."

They all broke out into laughter.

"Your tip is decreasing proportionately for every minute you laugh," I replied. "I think I might have the last laugh."

After they left, I ran my hand over the cool metal and traced many of the decorations with my fingertips. *What a spectacular piece of work,* I thought. *I will have this beauty here to look at every day. It is like owning my own art gallery. Think of the amount of time and effort that it took to create these images. What good is money if you don't spend it? No point in having any at all if you live like a pauper. Just the same, I probably need to watch it a bit.*

****

It was not possible to get the image of Elsie out of my mind. Thus it was not surprising that I felt compelled to visit the Lilly Store a couple of days later when I needed to purchase a shirt. I roamed around among the various dry good items until I spotted Elsie working at the check out counter. She was involved in helping a customer complete a purchase and looked just as lovely as she had when she stood at my store window.

I quickly grabbed a shirt that looked like it was approximately my size and approached the counter. I produced my best smile and said, "Good morning, Miss Corey."

"Hello, Mr. Swan. Please call me Elsie. How do you know my name?"

"George Volger who clerks at my store informed me. I was delighted to see you looking at my gems through the window the other day. Why didn't you come inside my shop?"

"Oh, Mr. Swan. I cannot afford to buy jewelry and I wouldn't want to waste your time nor the time of one of your clerks."

"Please call me Fitch, and I invite you to come for a tour. In fact, I will prepare a special tour for you at 2:00 tomorrow afternoon. You will be my guest and will not need to buy anything. It would be my pleasure to show you the items that I have on my shelves. There are diamonds and gems and sterling and silver watches, fine clocks and plated ware."

"I would be so honored by your kindness, Fitch."

****

My jewelry store clerks were to come an hour before we opened each day to discuss prospective delivery, repairs and plans. In the early morning meeting of the next day, I told them that I was going to have a special tour at 2:00 and I would appreciate their handling customers and business between 2:00 and 3:00.

"Do you mind if I ask who is coming?" asked my nephew Cornelius Cadle. When I told him that it would be Ms. Elsie Corey, he seemed very surprised. "Well, I thought it was going to be the President of the bank or some visiting dignitary or something," said Cornelius. "Doesn't she work across the street? Why is she having a tour? Is she considering working here? I think that would be great. We could use a woman's touch around here."

"Thank you, Cornelius but it is a personal matter and has nothing to do with working at the store," I said.

"I didn't think you were allowed to have any personal matters with young women."

"That will be enough. Let's get back to work. Customers will begin coming in the door any minute now."

I am certain that my employees noticed my increasing nervousness as 2:00 approached.

As I prepared tea, I began to be certain that she would not appear. After all, it is rather unusual for a young woman to have a tour of a store conducted by the proprietor. I should have thought of a better idea. She probably thinks I am a crazy old man at this point.

Just on the dot of 2:00, I heard the tinkling of the bell that was attached to my front door and in walked the lovely young lady. I hurried up front to greet her before Cornelius got a hold of her. "Hi, Elsie," I said. "Welcome to the Swan Jewelry Store."

"Thank you so much for your kindness, Fitch. I promise to not take up much of your time but I do so want to get a closer look at all of the beautiful items that you have."

"None are more beautiful than you," I said. What was I thinking? Why would I say such a thoughtless thing? Now she probably thinks I'm a crazy dirty old man.

Elsie blushed and looked down in response to my improper statement. It clearly made her nervous and her nervousness made me nervous and we ended up standing in a fretful silence. The quiet probably would have continued for the entire afternoon if it were not for George Volger. Cornelius was behind one of the display shelves towards the center of the store and was making a great effort to stifle his amusement. I could only see the back of George's head but it was clear that he was making fun of me.

I will not let him embarrass me, I thought. I asked Elsie if she would like to have a closer look at the amber in the window that had captured her interest yesterday.

"Actually," she said, "I absolutely love that clock. I have never seen such beautiful wood carving. Could I have a closer look?" I removed it from the window and sat it on a jewelry case. I wound it and set the time so that she could hear the resonance of its chimes. I showed her how there was a little hidden drawer in its back that housed its key. "It is very special, Fitch," she said. "Perhaps some day I could afford such a beautiful thing."

I took Elsie's arm and gently moved her behind the jewelry cases so that she could directly observe the gems in the built-in cases along the walls. She followed me around the store and marveled at the beauty of all of the stones. She obviously had an appreciation of all of my treasures, but remained quite reserved and formal throughout the visit.

****

It was when I took her to the back room to view my incredible safe that her reserve was lost.

Elsie's face lightened up and broke into a huge smile. "My word, Fitch, this is the most extraordinary thing that I have ever seen."

She began to laugh and I said, "I know, it is a bit too excessive for my back room, but I just had to have it once I saw it."

"I completely agree," she replied. "It is like owning an art gallery. If I owned that I would want to take it and place it right in the middle of my parlor so that I could see it every day."

It was then that I knew that Elsie and I belonged together.

The store tour was the beginning of the loving relationship that developed between us and that led to our wedding on the evening of May 29, 1907. We married at nine o'clock in the evening in the Baptist parsonage. (Muscatine Journal, May 30, 1907, pg 4) It is true that the brevity of our courtship and the modesty of our ceremony surprised many of my friends who had no idea that I had a lady in my life. I saw no need to put Elsie through the difficulties of obtaining their approval before our special day. I felt rather certain that they would not approve of me marrying so young a lady. They would not understand the complexity of our unique attraction.

I was overjoyed when Elsie said that she wanted to marry me. After all, I was thirty-two years her senior and she was one of the more popular young ladies of the city. She was a slender, petite woman with magnetic blue eyes and a thick, shiny mane of wavy brown locks but the characteristic that I found the most attractive was her delightful personality. I often told her in joking that she was a lovely young thing, emphasizing the fact that she was only 25 years old. My personal lack of confidence touched her and she responded by telling me that I was an exceptionally attractive entrepreneur. She said that my advancing years telegraphed power and strength and she did not mind that I was 57 years old.

I knew it was true when she said that I was attractive. I was fit and stylish for my age. My face was smooth with few wrinkles and my hair, although light gray was also thick and strong. I thought that my blue eyes actually were better accented when my hair turned gray so I grew a mustache to further enhance the effect. She was right when she told me that I didn't look a day over 40. I think it was the result of my artistic life.

When a man spends a lifetime around beautiful gems, appreciates gracious homes and lives with a beautiful woman, how could he help but to have that beauty reflected in himself?

I knew that my wealth and standing in the community initially influenced her marriage decision, but I feel confident that we also shared a great deal of affection, if not love. She cared for me and babied me.

An essential element was that she shared my artistic tastes. I cannot overstate the value of sharing the appreciation of beauty with a lady. We experienced the same delight in the wonder of the steam rising over the

Mississippi ice in January and awe at the splendor of the rise of the sun over its eastern banks. She was able to discern which gems would have the most value at my store. We could stand before the beauty of my safe and feel the same energy and excitement that only artists can understand.

Because of her aesthetic sensibilities, she decorated our home in a most pleasing fashion.

She spent a large portion of her time carefully planning for our future. In addition, Elsie constantly reflected my burning desire to have children. Her hopes for the future were completely harmonious with my own. She knew how to make me happy.

I had been nothing but thrilled to take good care of my beautiful Elsie in return. I knew how to treat and how to preserve gems. I provided her with household help, the best of attire and the company of the community's leaders. She had her pick of jewels and watches and she was thrilled on our wedding night to find that I had taken the oak clock that she so loved from the store and had placed it on a dresser in our bedroom.

****

Following our marriage, Elsie's Aunt Anna Fraleigh, moved into our home. Aunt Anna had actually raised Elsie and we both thought it reasonable that she occupy one of our many bedrooms. When Aunt Anna found the pantry in my kitchen to be regularly stocked with the widest range of staples, she went baking mad and she had a particular penchant for sweets. I enjoyed the constant smell of snickerdoodles, strudel and various German treats emanating from the kitchen but I became concerned with my inability to refrain from eating the sweets all of the time. It seemed as if every chair that I sat in had a bowl of cookies or candies within arm's reach. There was always the chocolate cake with the cream cheese frosting for dessert and then a special reward of an extra piece of pie before bedtime. Although Elsie and I were constantly drowning ourselves in these sugary delights, Elsie did not seem to gain a pound but my waist line began to balloon. I convinced Elsie that she needed to stop by the store every afternoon with a load of sweets that her Aunt had made in the morning. It could turn this potentially adverse situation into an advantage. Not only would my employees feel finely appreciated by my provision of such treats, but my customers would also find Swan's Jewelry to be an even more welcoming place to visit.

****

It was about this time when a clairvoyant named Harold Ulrich opened an establishment next to my own in the upper stair level. (Muscatine City Directory, January 1, 1908, pg 336) When I went over to greet him and welcome him to the business neighborhood, I scheduled a session with him on a lark. It seemed important to make certain that he knew that his efforts to establish a business were appreciated, even though there are many in the community that view such practices of clairvoyance and sooth-saying as the occupation of the slightly deranged.

I climbed the stairs to his business, knocked on the door and was welcomed inside. The room was dark, oppressive and smelled of incense. Harold had put heavy black-out drapes on all of the windows and had a little table set up in the middle of the rather empty room. He motioned for me to sit across from him, held both of my hands in his own and seemed to go into a kind of trance. After a few minutes he opened his eyes and stared at me solemnly. "Your future is full of sorrow, Fitch. You need a major change."

"Well, I have had a major change," I responded. "I just married a new wife."

"That will not be enough, Fitch; you need to leave this area."

I hastily thanked Harold, paid him and left. As I walked back to my store I reflected. *What nonsense. Everybody has sorrow in their future unless they die within the next day or two. He probably just wants me to move so that he can have my store location. How dumb does he think I am?*

Elsie Swan

Elsie Swan

It is odd what minor events end up having major consequences in our lives. I was simply walking along Second Street on the way to my job at Lilly's Dry Goods one day and noticed some activity in the window at Swan's Jewelry Store. I stopped to look without much thought when I observed the store proprietor, Fitch Swan himself, arranging jewelry around a large carved oak clock. It was fascinating to observe a man examining gems, picking them up and looking at them in the light, moving them to one location and then another until he found the most attractive placement. He moved around the display, viewing it from different heights and various angles until he got it in the most pleasing arrangement.

This is not the image of manhood that I have experienced in my life. Actually I have not had much of an image of manhood at all. The stories that I have heard from my mother and Aunt Anna indicate that my father was a rough, tough sort of man. He worked as a laborer in a saw mill and also as a miller and was a man who liked to hang out with the guys and have a few drinks. He was known to come stumbling and smashing into the house, striking at anything or anyone that got in his way. He had a wife and a family before he married my mother and will probably have wives and families after. My siblings and I were just a fragment of a long string of misery that he created in the world.

Father left my mother when I was about 2 years old. (1885 Iowa Census, Muscatine County) I have seen him here and there over the years, but have never thought it would be beneficial for me to attempt to develop any closeness with him. Don't get me wrong. I have wanted a father... actually longed for a father all of my childhood. I just don't want to invite sorrow into my life. It has provided enough misfortune on its own without me intentionally inviting any additional, unnecessary distress.

My father left my mother with nothing but debt. After much searching, she was finally able to obtain employment in the neighboring small town of Wilton. She could not work all day and also care for me and my brother John and sister Daisy. Her low wages did not allow her to hire good care for us children and she felt uneasy about the kind of parenting that we would receive from the hands of strangers. She therefore left us in the care of our Aunt Anna in Muscatine.

Aunt Anna Fraleigh

My brother, sister and I lived a humble life in Aunt Anna's small box of a home on East 5th Street, east of the business district. (Muscatine City Directory, January 1, 1907, pg 66) Aunt Anna was a German lady who did her best to provide a warm and comfortable home for us. She loved to knit, tat and crochet and attempted to make our home look attractive with her doilies and throws.

My aunt also believed strongly in discipline and obedience, being on time, respect for elders, following rules. She was a kind and loving lady as long as you behaved in a way that she viewed as proper. Although she was strict and exacting, I also knew that she was dependable and would stay with me and not desert me. Aunt Anna provided the only stability and security that I experienced during my childhood. Over time, my relationship with my mother diminished and I identified Aunt Anna as my mother.

She loved to cook and to bake her traditional German dishes when she could afford to purchase the ingredients. Many times we were provided with simple but tasty meals. These more modest meals were supplemented with a large bowl of biscuits or rolls in the middle of the table. When there was not enough money for meat or expensive fruits and vegetables, we could always fill up with the rolls. Although some meals consisted only of those rolls, split and filled with jam, we never went hungry.

Aunt Anna was always nervous about my relationships with males. She reminded me repeatedly that my father was, "no good", "irresponsible" and "undisciplined". She had the unfortunate view that the only worthwhile people were those of German origin. I recall the constant refrain "drunken Irishman" from her in respect to my father.

She was therefore motivated to skeptically eye every male who came within ten feet of me even when I was a young child in grade school. She regularly took me to church and reminded me to "act like a child of Jesus" whenever a boy was near.

It surprised me to find that I was rather popular among the boys. I think it was because I have had little of the female subtlety or refinement. When I am around other people, I look them directly in the eye and attempt to hear all that they say and to understand the nuances of meaning through their gestures and expressions. I have never been able to assume the goodness in people, nor that they intend to fulfill their obligations and roles in society or to me.

A child of violence must always keep watch. This is particularly true of violence which is not connected to the behavior of the child, but which is the result of the irrational impulses of the adult. Since the aggression was not attached to any behaviors on my part, there was nothing that I could do to stop or decrease it. I learned to constantly scan the environment to detect unexpected movements on the part of others.

****

You can imagine the reaction of Aunt Anna when, upon arriving home, I informed her that Fitch Swan the jeweler had invited me for a personal tour of his store the next day. "Oh, Elsie. Be careful. What is this man up to?"

"I think he just wants for me to see his store. I don't see how that means that he is up to anything," I replied.

"It is not good for a man to give you such special attention, Elsie."

"He saw me observing him placing jewels in his window, appreciated my interest and wants me to be able to have a good look at them."

"Why would a man of his means be interested in showing you his jewels?"

"Oh, Aunt Anna, he is just being nice."

"Don't be foolish, Elsie, men are not that nice."

"Perhaps Fitch Swan is that nice, Aunt Anna. I intend to find out."

****

Aunt Anna was nervously waiting for me at the door when I arrived home the next day. "Was he a gentleman, Elsie?"

I told her about the store and the clocks, watches and gems. I tried to explain how thoughtful and kind Fitch Swan was to me. I described the beautiful safe with all of its artistry surrounding the phrase "Love is a Cottage".

"Love is a Cottage. What does that mean, Elsie?"

"I think that it means that the people in a cottage or in a home are what represent the love in our lives. The emphasis is that it is the people and not the wealth that brings meaning into our lives. I think that only a thoughtful man would select a safe with such a saying."

"Does it seem odd that they would put that on a very expensive, ornately embellished safe that is made to keep money and material goods secure?" asked Aunt Anna.

"Let's not over-think this," I replied.

****

The following week, Fitch walked me to a lunch at Leu's Confectioners which was a few blocks from our stores. We strolled up and down the street with World's Fair Cornucopias made of ice cream scooped into waffles rolled into cone shapes. We laughed at the difficulty of consuming these treats before the ice cream soaked through the waffle and onto our clothing and joked about what people would think of us at the end of our walk when we were covered with food.

Fitch mentioned that people would probably not approve of someone of his age associating in such an intimate setting with someone of my age anyway. "Intimate setting, Fitch? You think of walking through the center of downtown at noon as an intimate setting?"

Fitch laughed. "There is always somebody who will criticize about anything," he replied.

In reality, I think that Fitch would be quite surprised to know of the attraction that I felt for him because of his age. His age signaled to me that he had proven through the years that he was reliable and dependable. He had established a successful marriage and a thriving and profitable business. He was highly respected by community members. I could not have found anybody in the town that more exemplified the "timeliness, tidiness and trustworthiness" that Aunt Anna always emphasized.

Fitch's economic well-being was not of much importance in itself. What was important to me was the security that the wealth could provide for me, Aunt Anna and any children that might be in my future. It was not the shiny jewels and the fancy china that I found attractive. It was the stability and the security that existed in his life. His assets could keep away hunger and coldness. They could keep the wolf away from my door for the rest of my life.

We so enjoyed each other's company during that lunch, that we went to dinner at the Crown Restaurant on Iowa Avenue a few days later. When Fitch dropped me off afterward he spent some time with my Aunt Anna who was absolutely smitten by the gentlemanly and impeccably groomed Mr. Swan. He easily fulfilled her checklist of life's important qualities. After he left our home, Aunt Anna joked, "If you don't want to continue to see him, Elsie, I will."

Now that I had Aunt Anna's approval of Fitch, my feelings for him increased rapidly. He soon invited us to visit his residence on the top of the bluffs on East Third Street. We arrived by horse and buggy and were amazed at the beauty of his home. Aunt Anna spent most of the visit looking through the windows at the various views of the Mississippi that were visible from this home on the top of the hill. "This is a good place," she said, "Elsie, this is a good man."

****

Before long, Fitch asked me to marry him and said that he thought that Aunt Anna should live with us. When he hired men to move our belongings to our new location, Aunt Anna and I were rather uncomfortable to observe them pack and move our belongings. We both lived in a world where you completed your own jobs. If it needed to be done, you figured out how to do it. It was such a strange feeling to watch as others performed all of the heavy and difficult tasks.

I attempted to settle into the home and to make it my own. I moved furniture around and exchanged the items on some tables with the items on others. Meanwhile, Aunt Anna scurried all about the home arranging her doilies and throws throughout the residence. Even though it most certainly did not fit with Fitch's aesthetics, he praised Aunt Anna and remarked on the beauty of the items and told her that he was going to send her with the housekeeper in the next few days to purchase all of the yarn and crochet thread that she needed.

When Aunt Anna walked into the kitchen pantry, she had to sit down for a while. The shelves of the large room were covered with spices and all kinds of cooking supplies as well as glassware and china. It was a virtual heaven to her. She placed her apron around her middle, stoked up the oven and began baking. She baked nearly all day every day and we ended up with such an excessive amount of sweet treats around the house that Fitch became concerned about our ability to keep up with the flow. He suggested that I take most of each day's output to the store in the afternoons. This seemed like a wonderful idea to me. Since I married Fitch, I had resigned from my job and was now missing the constant daily human interaction to which I had become accustomed. This would provide me an opportunity to visit with Fitch, his employees and some of his customers on a regular basis. This would be great.

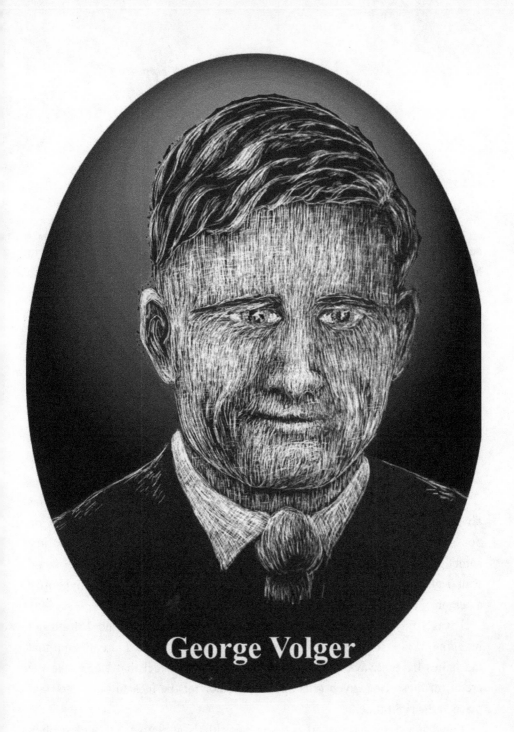

George Volger

George Volger

I have just learned that my boss Fitch Swan has married Elsie Corey. I actually read about it in the paper, as did most of Muscatine. This appears to have been a rather rushed, secretive event that occurred at 9:00 at night in the parsonage. Clearly there is something wrong with this picture.

My concern has been growing ever since Mr. Swan provided a private tour of the jewelry store to this young lady who is actually only a few years older than I. I am not certain for whom to have the most concern, Mr. Swan or Elsie. Is it proper for a man of Fitch Swan's age to have a relationship with a girl of Elsie's age? Does anybody actually think that Elsie is attracted to anything more than his wealth? This whole situation speaks of sinister motivations to me.

****

Elsie was a few years ahead of me in school and I can tell you that she was always in a cluster of boys. They were attracted to her like bees to honey. I am not saying that she ever did anything wrong mind you. There was just something about her. She wasn't shy and coy like the other girls. She would walk right up to you and look straight into your eyes and practically hypnotize a person.

I was a big time athlete and the most popular boy in the school. I am not bragging. It is just a fact that I can play about any sport that I attempt and that the ladies have always been attracted to me. I don't feel that I can take the credit for these God given gifts and talents, nor for the luck to be in the right place at the right time.

I have never viewed myself as being particularly attractive, although women have described me as tall, dark and handsome. I am fit and muscular because I play ball and exercise so often. Of course my wife, Helen, tells me I am handsome all of the time.

I am presently employed as a clerk at the Swan Jewelry Store. I became acquainted with Mr. Swan in the course of my athletic endeavors. He has always been a supporter of local ball teams and has donated many items to the teams. So when I was 16 years old and I was looking for a job he offered to train me in the fields of jewelry making and time piece repair. It was not exactly the career that I anticipated but I found that I had a lot of natural ability and I derived great enjoyment from the work.

The social interaction in retail was a factor that I had underestimated in my career plans. When my team members, friends and sports fans in the community discovered that I was working at Swan's, they frequented the establishment. Some came just to chat, but many found things that they decided to buy when they visited. It wasn't long before my presence began to increase the profits of the store. The fact that I could be a benefit to Mr. Swan was very gratifying to me. He had reached out to help me when I needed a job and now I could provide some compensation to him.

Social life in the establishment was also made interesting by the presence of Cornelius who, like me, was a clerk in training, as well as the nephew of Mr. Swan. Cornelius was a very hard working and capable artisan who taught me many things about jewels and metals. He had a great sense of humor and was constantly cracking jokes that were often at the expense of Mr. Swan, who seemed to have real affection for Cornelius and certainly exhibited a great deal of tolerance toward him.

Cornelius Cadle

The fact of the matter is that Cornelius could be very annoying. He was a man who was rather small in stature and who had a quick and uncontrollable temper. When things did not go as he wanted, his face would turn red, his eyes would begin to bulge and an explosion would commence. He would bounce up and down in his chair, pound on the work bench and raise his voice to an improper level. On many occasions, Mr. Swan would come out of his office and say, "Okay, Cornelius. Whatever the problem is, let us calm down and talk about it like rational people."

Cornelius and I developed a strategy to help him control his temper. Every time he began to feel anger, he was to look at me and nod and I would make a funny face at him. This could interrupt the build up of his emotions with the use of humor. I did not know if it would work but it seemed like it might lessen his stress. As a result of this plan, he would constantly nod at me, I would make a face and he would respond with laughter. Although it did not take long for me to realize that this approach was not productive, it began a regular practice of foolery between Cornelius and myself that was probably not beneficial to the business.

****

Elsie's first visit to the store caused Cornelius to become anxious. His anxiety was not triggered so much by bad things or good things, but was a result of new and different things. He apparently had not thought of his Uncle Swan as a person who entertains young ladies. In our conversations about this new behavior, we both agreed to be quiet, listen and watch closely and to use Cornelius' stress relieving technique if he became agitated. We would have a quiet conference afterwards to assess the situation.

It was immediately clear that Mr. Swan was attracted to Elsie. He actually fixed a cup of tea for her. Cornelius became quite anxious and, as a result,

43

giggled nervously through the entire visit like a complete fool. I was particularly concerned when they took their tea into the back room and spent considerable time talking softly and laughing amongst themselves.

Cornelius and I were both troubled about the possibility that Elsie was playing with the sentiments of Mr. Swan. He had experienced the loss of his wife recently and the loss of a newborn a few years earlier and he was at a vulnerable point in his life. We agreed that it was appropriate for him to seek female companionship but it needed to be with a woman nearer to his own age who could understand his life experiences and losses and who could take care of him. Elsie did not fit this description.

You can imagine my surprise when I read of their marriage in the Journal. Some time had elapsed since that first meeting and they obviously had been courting. It is clear that Cornelius has known about the progression of the relationship and has been told to not discuss it with me. I guess it really is none of my business but I feel a bit offended that I was not invited to the wedding. However, it does look like it was a very small affair. Perhaps I am being too sensitive. Mr. Swan has always been a good employer to me.

Chapter 2: 1908 to 1912
Fitch Swan

In the early years of our marriage, I expanded the products sold in the store to include fountain pens, cut glass, handbags, fine umbrellas and purses, as well as silver plated flatware. This was, of course, in addition to the very best jewelry, watches and clocks. My profits continued to increase and the store ran smoothly.

Everything in my life was moving in a positive direction with the exception of my relationship with George Volger. I liked George, but he was becoming increasingly annoying. Last year he began touring the United States with the Tourists, Muscatine's basketball team that had won the world championship. This has caused him to need many absences from his responsibilities at the store. I am aware that the world of sports is important in his life, but I have a business to run and I need for my employees to respect the importance of that endeavor.

He also has a tendency to spend too much time entertaining the customers rather than making sales to them. I realize that he attracts many of the people into the store and that a lot of this attraction is because of his athletic popularity, but I hired him to spend the majority of his time working and not socializing.

Although I have spoken to George about the lack of completion of his assigned tasks, I was not deeply concerned because my nephew Cornelius took up the slack. A harder working young man than Cornelius was never created and he is also highly skilled with a good eye for design and detail.

George did not seem to be able to respect my boundaries. He was accustomed to being the center of attention because of his sports success. There are increasing periods of time when I would find myself working at various tasks while George socialized with the customers about sports. The situation became completely intolerable when he crossed the boundaries of my relationship with Elsie.

When Elsie made her daily pastry deliveries to the store, George attempted to monopolize her time and attention. There simply was no end to the topics that he needed to discuss with her. On one such afternoon, Elsie came rushing excitedly into the store, held up a dirty little stone and exclaimed,

"Look at what I found at the river, Fitch. What is it? See all of the stripes of color. Isn't it about the most beautiful thing you have ever seen?"

I picked up the stone and examined it closely. "It is a Lake Superior agate, Elsie. One can find them occasionally along the river. They came to this area through glacial drift."

"Would you please make me a pendant out of it? I would love to have a pendant of a jewel that I have found right here on the shores of the Mississippi."

"Well, Elsie, it is not exactly a jewel and I think I can detect a crack running through it. It is hardly a precious stone and is not really of enough value to wear as a pendant."

At that point George broke into our conversation and said, "Give it to me, Elsie. I will take care of it."

A week later George presented Elsie with a golden pendant inset with a polished slice of the agate. Elsie was delighted and immediately put it on and exclaimed that it was the most beautiful necklace she had ever received. She thanked George numerous times and wore that necklace for several weeks, until I told her that I would appreciate a little variety in her jewelry attire. After all, she is the wife of a jeweler and the community always takes notice of the jewelry that she wears.

****

My business was proving very profitable during this period of time and therefore I was quite agreeable in 1908 when Cornelius mentioned that he had been dreaming of owning his own store. He said that he was getting to the age where he felt he needed to advance his career. I understood his desire to achieve a higher standard of living and supported him in his establishment of a new jewelry store that was located a block up the street from my own at 109 East Second Street. (January 1, 1908 Muscatine City Directory, pg 352) I was glad to be able to assist him in ensuring that his store had adequate stock.

Since I have never had a child of my own, Cornelius has occupied a special

46

place in my heart. As soon as he first learned to walk, he would hold out his arms and toddle precariously toward me when I came through the door of his home. My heart would fill with joy as I scooped him up and sat him on my shoulders. I would spend hours being my little Cornelius' pony, trotting around the neighborhoods.

He was such a child of joy that I am afraid that he was rarely disciplined. He had a proclivity for throwing little tantrums. When he did not have his needs met, his face would redden, he would clasp his hands into tight fists and he would scream with such ferocity that his entire body would seem to levitate. All of the adults in his life found this behavior to be so cute and humorous that we failed to intervene. As a result, to this day, Cornelius has difficulty when things do not go exactly his way. Although it stopped being cute a long time ago, it seems that all of the adults did not respond appropriately at a young enough age to modify the behavior. It has continued to provide him with problems throughout his adult life.

Thus when Cornelius wanted to open his own business, I was pleased to support the dear young man, but I was concerned about his ability to manage a business effectively. There is much emotional control involved in business and particularly in a retail establishment. There often is not an opportunity to step away and calm oneself when necessary. Unfortunately my concerns were proven to be accurate.

Cornelius found it impossible to maintain profitability. Although his craftsmanship was of the highest level, his temperament tended to drive employees and customers away. The stress of the challenge of developing and sustaining a new retail establishment increased his anxiety problems at the times when his business required that they be at a low level for its success. After three years he expressed a need to drastically alter his financial plan. My beloved sister Harriet, Cornelius' mother, pleaded with me to help Cornelius out of his difficult situation. She hinted that my new community clock was responsible for the decline of his business.

****

In January of 1911, I had sought permission from the city council to donate a huge 30 day timepiece to the city, to be erected on the sidewalk on East Second Street in front of my store. I had it installed right next to the curb, as close to the street as I could get. Nobody traveling down Second Street from either direction could miss that. It is marketing genius... ever present, continual advertising. Every time anybody sees that clock they will think of me and of my generosity. They will remember that I have always made every effort to beautify this community.

I had the clock delivered to the council room on January 25. Its enormity made it difficult to transport the large timepiece to the chambers without a lot of heaving and pushing but it made quite a startling impression on all to see it enter and tower in place over the assembly. An amused Muscatine Journal reporter was present at the time and he wrote, "Today (Fitch Swan) brought a large 30-day clock to the city hall and it has already been placed in the council chamber. The donation is indeed a timely one and will be greatly appreciated by the councilmen. That the presence of the timepiece will promote dispatch on the part of the members of that body when in session is the devout wish of everyone who is forced to worry through the long evening when the feasibility and advisability of placing a board walk on some street in the environs of the city is a momentous question under discussion. ...That the clock is ashamed because of its present surroundings is evidenced by the fact that it has kept its hands in front of its face ever since taken into the room. At the next meeting it is thought that that timepiece will pass on its first reading". (The Muscatine Journal, January 25, 1911, pg 7, "PLACE TIMEPIECE IN COUNCIL ROOM")

There are those, in addition to my sister Harriet, who say that my street clock installation was so successful that I drained the business right out of the downtown. People were drawn from Cornelius' business to my own because of the ever present advertisement. I don't think that is true but it did increase my motivation to help Cornelius find a way out of his dilemma.

****

I devised a plan. I would bring Cornelius and his stock back into my store which we would advertise as a 'merger' and 'consolidation' (The Muscatine Journal, April 11, 1911, Advertisement, pg 4) and I would encourage George to buy the fixtures and begin his own business in Cornelius' vacant store. Through this plan, I could provide support and protection for my nephew and get George out from under my roof in a way that would offer future opportunity to him. I am sure that the big time athlete will have no problem competing with my clock.

Therefore in May of 1911 Cornelius and I advertised that he was in the process of consolidating his stock with mine. He moved back into my store

48

with all of the jewelry and watches. George purchased Cornelius' fixtures and opened his own store in June in that location along with many accolades in the local press. It was stressed by the media that he had a special popularity among the younger social sets of the community because of his prominence as an athlete on the basketball court. I recognized the appreciation of athletics in the community but did not see how it had much of a relationship with the jewelry and clock making business. I was certain that the excitement would subside.

During that year I participated in a trade excursion with the Muscatine Boosters to advertise the greatness of this city. I have so often emphasized Muscatine's successes and its future of prosperity. I declared to the media that "Muscatine looks better to me on that day than at any time in its history". I stated that, "Since I entered business in this city until the present day Muscatine has gradually improved until today it is the finest city in the state in which to live Our prospects of a brilliant future have never been as bright as they are now. Everyone is prospering and the scarcity of labor will be impressed upon anyone who endeavors to find a man who is sufficiently at liberty to perform some odd jobs. Everybody who wants to work has been given steady employment and they are getting good wages too. Living expenses are twenty-five percent cheaper than in towns of corresponding size. No one realizes just how fine Muscatine is until after a resident born here leaves for some other point". (The Muscatine Journal, May 5, 1910, pg 1, "TRADE EXCURSIONISTS OFF ON BIG BOOSTER TRIP")

My enthusiasm for those affirmative declarations began to lessen as I observed the increasing level of traffic in George's store and the decreasing level in my own. The constantly improving profit levels of my store began to decline. My initial conclusion was that the paper had been correct and that the ebb in sales was due to the novelty to the community of the popular 'athletic star' opening a business. I knew that people in small town Iowa are historically nosey and are used to having intimate knowledge of the activities of their neighbors. It seemed obvious that once they have visited George's store and have looked it over, the customer level would drop.

As the summer waned and the holiday season approached, I decided that I needed to put extra emphasis on my experience and dependability in order to increase the holiday traffic. Surely people would prefer to do their business with me when their thoughts are focused in the right direction?

On the 19th of December I made arrangements with the Journal to run "Remember Swan is the most reliable Jeweler in Muscatine. 44th YEAR IN

BUSINESS at the top of my advertisement. Swan leads in the Jewelry trade. Two large stocks to select from and the most new goods". (The Muscatine Journal, December 19, 1911, pg 6, Swan Advertisement) I was pleased with myself after I read a mock-up of the ad for approval. This was exactly what I needed to do. It would put people's thoughts on the right track before they decided on their Christmas purchases. I was also amused at the thought of the discomfort that Volger would feel when he read the ad. There was just no way that he could deny the fact that my experience outstrips him by many years.

The next afternoon I actually felt some excitement when the Journal was delivered to my store. I picked up the paper and scanned through the pages until I got to the advertising section. There at the top of the page in the desirable above-the-fold location, on the far right, was my good sized ad. It was wonderful.

Wait a minute...

There at the bottom of the page was a picture of George Volger. The photo and its central location caused it to be more noticeable than all other advertisements even though it was smaller in size than most. It stated "See me before buying. You are assured of new goods when you buy your XMAS Gifts at Volger's NEW JEWELRY STORE. Prices always right. Store open evenings". (The Muscatine Journal, December 19, 1911, pg 6, Volger Advertisement)

Good Lord, what is that boy attempting to insinuate? Is he saying that I do not purchase new stock? Is he trying to make the fact that my store has been open for many years, a defect? When he has been in business the number of years that I have been in business he also will have things that he has purchased previously that were overstocked and that he will have to sell.

What does he expect me to do with it all? They are 'new' items in the sense that they have never been used or worn. The fact that they were designed in prior years and that they have sat on my shelves for some time has no relevance whatsoever. I buy some new stock every year also. I don't have to buy the quantity of new items that he does because I am not just opening the business. Has the man never heard of the concept of inventory? He is just displaying his ignorance for the whole world to see. I think he has been hit in the head by too many basketballs!

****

Weeks went by and the business at my store did not reach its normal holiday season pitch. I kept a close eye on the Volger property. Although I usually had an employee shovel the snow off the sidewalks, I began to shovel myself so that I could watch the traffic going through George's store. It was constant and heavy. I noted that many of the customers were people associated with the community ball teams. Some were also my own.

Christmas came and went and my store's sales were well below its usual holiday seasonal level. Volger has the sports community all wrapped up and has gotten a ton of publicity through his participation in sports. I need to get my name before the public more often. I have donated to this community in various ways for many years. I need to step it up and make them remember that I have supported them and that they need to support me in return.

Although I still felt relatively certain that my sales would rebound within the next year, I devised a brilliant marketing plan to ensure that the community was regularly reminded of my presence. I had donated loving cups to the city basketball league for several years. I need to remind the local sports community that I have always been an avid fan. I have supported them in the past and they need to support me now.

I will donate an even bigger and better cup this year. For the fourth consecutive year I donated a large, silver loving-cup to the victors of the factory basketball league tourney played at the Y.M.C.A. The trophy stood twelve inches high and was to be engraved with the names of the players of the winning team. I displayed it in the window of my store for all to come and see and also planned to award it personally. The community was excited about this tournament and it was expected that the largest crowd of the season would attend the game. Surely this would get more people into the store and while there they might make some purchases?

The slow but steady decline in my business continued. The holidays passed. There was a burst of activity in the sale of wedding and engagement rings in the spring during bridal season. I was accustomed to practicing some endurance over the summer season due to the fact that other than an occasional wedding, engagements and scattered birthdays, few jewels were purchased in the summer. I was kept afloat by the repair and sale of clocks and watches. People wanted to be able to know the time all throughout the year.

****

I believe that the occurrence of the Button Strike that began in February (Annals of Iowa, Volume 46, Issue 4 (spring 1982) The Muscatine Button Workers'

Strike of 1911-12, Kate Rousmaniere, pgs 243-262) greatly impacted the behavior of my customers. Muscatine has been considered the button production capital of the world since mussels with pearlescent interiors were found in the Mississippi River around 1891.

Of course, the workers formed a union after the businesses began to prosper to ensure that they were getting their share of the wealth. We business people have to expect this behavior and the union threat caused little concern because of its limited power until 1910 when it affiliated with the American Federation of Labor. (The Muscatine Journal, October 28, 1910, pg 5, "BUTTON WORKERS FORMING A UNION")

I am well informed of the details of this struggle due to the fact that I was asked to be on a committee of businessmen which was formed for the purpose of mediating between the involved parties. I can tell you that the button companies had to shut down operation this year and lay off workers because the demand for buttons has declined. The fact that the unions considered this action to be a lockout in response to their federal affiliation is hard to comprehend since there has been much coverage in the newspapers of garment strikes all over the nation. Any observant and reasoning individual should be able to conclude that less garments produced equals less buttons needed. It is an easy mathematical formula to comprehend.

At the same time that the manufacturers were doing all that they could to raise the button orders and optimize the environment of the workers, the workers themselves were sneaking around behind their backs and plotting to unionize and working on an effort to demand a wage raise of 25 to 100%.

I actually toured some factories where the owners built pleasant lunch rooms fitted out with such things as $35 coffee boilers (The Muscatine Journal, April 27, 1911, pg 5, "DR. BATTEN TELLS OF BUTTON STRIKE") for the convenience and pleasure of the workers only to find that the workers refused to use the facilities because they did nothing to meet their demands for higher pay and union representation. It is clear to see why the owners came to the logical conclusion that they had spoiled the employees with too generous treatment. They had made a mistake in the past by paying too high wages in Muscatine and treating the employees with too great liberality.

The union was unwilling to compromise and protested in a strike of such a violent nature that the factories, as well as the community itself, were threatened. The unionists intimidated workers who passed the picket line to fulfill their responsibility to those who had provided them with a living. In addition, they threw rocks and bricks into the homes of some of them. It was eventually necessary for the sheriff to call in a police force from Chicago and St. Louis in order to protect our citizens. (Annals of Iowa, Volume 46, Issue 4 (spring 1982) The Muscatine Button Workers' Strike of 1911-12, Kate Rousmaniere, pgs 243-262)

The button workers responded with a city wide riot that was composed of about 5,000 unionists that threatened the safety of the special police force. Of course, the militia was eventually called in and martial law declared to obtain control over these ungrateful ruffians. (Annals of Iowa, Volume 46, Issue 4 (spring 1982) The Muscatine Button Workers' Strike of 1911-12, Kate Rousmaniere, pgs 243-262)

Although the militia was able to restore peace after 4 days and the public fury subsided by the beginning of 1912, my customer base was made uneasy by the commotion on the streets. The people who benefit most from my store are the business people, factory owners, leaders and decent law-abiding citizens of this community. During this conflict and for a considerable time afterward they were hesitant to appear on the streets or in the stores for fear of the reaction of the rabble. These individuals attempt to avoid trouble and do not feel comfortable on the streets in dangerous situations such as this.

Many of my customers are also the more senior members of our community. They were repelled by the sight of armed police patrols and union thugs milling about the streets. They were able to achieve their advanced years because of a sensitivity and aversion to dangerous situations. The loss of the consistency of their continuous consumer loyalty caused my sales to decline considerably.

****

Swan Home: Sheltering Oaks

It may be hard to believe but in spite of this increasing financial concern, I found it necessary to build a new home. Early in our marriage, Elsie began expressing the desire to have a home of her own. Although she and Anna made every effort to alter our present home to fit her standards, she continued to have the sense that this was Mollie's home. It seemed to particularly bother her that Mollie died in the bedroom that she and I now share. She is not able to move beyond that.

It took me some time to accept the fact that I would need to give up my neighborhood with its shady elms and scenic views over the river. When I reminded Elsie that our present home was so convenient to my store that I could walk to work, she said, "For heaven's sake, Fitch, you have a Cadillac and a chauffeur. I think you will be able to get to your store from wherever we move." She had a point.

After touring several lots in the process of being developed in the new Fair Oaks division of the community, I found an area that I assessed to be the most beautiful location in the city. In 1910 I purchased two of the choicest lots in Fair Oaks and had a rambling 2 story home built across from the largest park in the area. (The Muscatine Journal, February 23, 1910, pg 4, "FW Swan buys two lots in

Fair Oaks") It is a delightful place with a porch that curves around the front and a balcony outside of our upstairs bedroom. It is one of the most beautiful homes in Muscatine, perched on the hill of the most scenic park.

The park sits on the rolling bluffs of the Mississippi on a spot that signified such spirituality that the Native Americans of the area built their burial mounds upon it. I found that Elsie and I could stand next to those mounds, on the crest of the hill and observe the Mississippi snaking far below as it worked its way through the trees and the underbrush. It moved relentlessly onward. How could she possibly not feel the love?

****

Following the move it became apparent that there was a need to increase the fire protection for my home and the other structures in my new neighborhood. My long involvement in efforts to protect the community from the constant threat of fire peaked in the establishment of the Alert Hose Company, one of the local volunteer fire-fighting groups in Muscatine. We obtained the permission of the City Council to rent a building to house the 'hose cart' that was to be used in the East Hill area. (The Muscatine Journal, October 19, 1911, pg 10, "ALERTS MEET AT THE CLUBHOUSE")

I was excited about participation in this organization. Fires were a serious threat to the community. All heating systems operated through the burning of coal or wood. Fireplaces were plentiful and were viewed as very effective in heating the area of the homes in which people gathered to a comfortable degree. In addition, all homes had kerosene lamps and candles for use during the many power outages. Many people, such as Elsie, preferred to turn off the lights during the cold gray winter days and to light candles instead. The candles produced a soothing, soft glow and projected a feeling of coziness and warmth into the rooms. It made the homes feel welcoming and hospitable when one came in from the frozen, harsh reality of the out-of-doors in Iowa in the wintertime All of these activities, of course, caused a bit of a fire hazard.

Elsie therefore expressed some relief when I told her about the planned hose company. She hoped I and the neighborhood would have it fully developed and operational by Christmas because she always experienced a bit of stress when she decorated the home for that holiday. Although she used candles at Halloween, the Fourth of July and Easter, she really went all out at Christmas time. She had a huge fir tree placed in the parlor each year and covered it with hundreds of candles placed in small drip catchers that clipped to the branches. I always joked that she was creating a forest fire but I also enjoyed the display. Our favorite evening was to sit at the fireplace together and to drink Christmas peppermint tea while the tree blazed in all of its glory.

She suggested to me, "Please mention to the Alert Hose group, the next time that you meet, that we need to have a huge party to celebrate the opening of the new hose facility." She was so grateful for the efforts of the men involved that she was quite willing to devote her time for its organization. "I will send invitations and organize the food. I will gather a group of East Hill ladies to plan the decorations and the activities. We can have games and maybe even some dancing."

I have been involved in the organization of a hook and ladder company since 1877 when I was elected as assistant captain of ladders and as a member of the standing committee. (The Muscatine Journal, April 13, 1917, pg 3, "FORTY YEARS AGO") An organizational meeting of the new company took place on the 15th of December at the park next to my home. The notion of the party planning caused a heated exchange among members who felt a need to make certain that all involved knew that this was not just another community social group. They diplomatically voted to postpone the celebration until after the holidays.

Instead, we proceeded to Park Avenue in order to become familiar with the operation of the hose cart. Quite a crowd of amused onlookers gathered to watch as we grabbed a hold of the cart and ran down the street at top speed. Although I was much older than the majority of the men, it felt good to me to run with them, while clutching the cart. I could actually keep up with most of them.

Of course there were always those 'show-offs' that must run ahead of everybody else. This was just another example of how age was an advantage. You never make friends by beating them at the assigned task and running ahead of them. You have your greatest influence on others if you calibrate your advances with theirs, by running beside them, not in back or in front. It occurred to me that I would be running much faster when a neighborhood house was on fire and the lives of its inhabitants threatened. This seemed like a critically important activity to me and I was glad when it was decided that the group would meet every Tuesday and Thursday to become familiar with the nuances of the operation of the hose cart.

Elsie Swan

I enjoyed delivering pastries to Fitch's store in the afternoons. I actually did not manage to find the time to make daily deliveries but was able to furnish the store with the pastries that our home did not consume one or two times a week. Although I had every intention of directing most of my attention to Fitch, my focus seemed to be increasingly captured by George Volger. His charm and attractiveness made him difficult to ignore. He had the 'gift of the gab' and seemed to be able to chat on and on about any subject. He liked to discuss social issues and politics with me, which is something that Fitch was reluctant to do.

Fitch favored a peaceful and serene home life. He did not like to see the 'waters roiled' regarding most issues. I respected his point of view, his efforts to get along with others and his appreciation of life from a rational rather than an emotional viewpoint. He preferred things to be organized, analyzed, and optimized. I seldom focused on issues that would upset him and saved expression of my more radical viewpoints for George, who often agreed with my opinions.

There was one occasion in particular that I knew upset Fitch. One day I found a lovely, glistening, striped stone lying on the banks of the Mississippi. I picked it up and was amazed by the hues that existed within its striations. I am excited by items of such beauty that have been created by the earth. I rushed into the store with the stone to show it to Fitch and asked him to make it into a pendant for me.

Fitch, with his usual logic and disciplined judgment stated that the stone was not of sufficient value to wrap with gold or silver and wear as a pendant. George saw my emotion and understood my disappointment. He hastily picked up the stone and said that he would take care of it. A few days later he presented me with the most beautiful pendant of his own creation. I appreciated his efforts and wore the pendant daily until Fitch indicated that it was an annoyance to him. In retrospect I am glad that this occurred because it made me aware that underneath his serene and positive exterior, some negative emotion such as jealousy could exist.

I attempted to convince Fitch that he was the number one priority of my life. He had told me about the loss of the child at birth that he and Mollie had anticipated. Fitch was a child magnet. He constantly bounced young boys up on his shoulders and danced around with them. I cautioned him that serious problems could result if he happened to drop one of these dear little beings while in the course of all of the frivolity. He was, however, unable to prevent himself and his nephew, Cornelius told me of how he always waited for his Uncle Fitch to visit so that he could get his ride. Apparently this is a practice in long standing.

I focused on efforts to have a child for Fitch and myself during this time. It was surprising to me that it did not occur within the first year of marriage. I tried various types of tea and herbal supplements to induce pregnancy. I charted my 'cycle' and made sure that I ate well and got plenty of rest at just the right times. There was no success at this point and I became concerned but Fitch told me to relax. He said that these things came naturally and that he was certain that we would have 4 or 5 little ones running around the house before long. Fitch said that this might provide an outlet for Aunt Anna's 'pastry problem'.

As I found my desires increasingly focused upon home and family, I came to the realization that I wanted a home of my own. I wished for a large and rambling space with a big yard and a park for the children across the street. It needed to be located in a neighborhood where I was not constantly being compared to Mollie.

The love that the neighbors had for Mollie, unfortunately created distress for me. I was making a serious effort to be the kind of lady that the community expected as the wife of Fitch Swan but I knew that I was being compared to her and that I was coming up short. Although the ladies were always polite and kind to me, I knew in my heart that I was a disappointment. I lacked the social graces and social standing of Mollie. I was aware that they thought I was too young for Fitch and I could overhear in their whispers that they thought I was only attracted to his money. All maintained very formal relations with me and none were interested in making a close friendship with me.

I wanted to start family life in a new neighborhood with new chances. I needed a neighborhood that was not so intimately familiar with Mollie Swan. I needed to define my own space and my own home. Even though I was young, I had faith that I could learn to be a proper wife for the community leader.

We reviewed every available site in the community for several months before we found the perfect spot right across the street from the most beautiful park in the city. When Fitch identified the location of the Indian burial grounds in the center of the park, I felt certain that the heavens were directing me to this magical location. We designed and built the most exquisite home that the world has ever seen. It was surrounded by stately oak trees and we therefore named it Sheltering Oaks. I truly felt that it would shelter my hopes and dreams for the future.

Fitch soon became concerned about my safety in the new location that was further removed from the store than our old home. Since fires were a particular worry in our community, he helped to organize a new fire company. He wanted to make certain that assistance to my home would be available within the shortest time possible. He became very involved in the group and practiced with them often. I offered to organize a grand opening party for the new facility. I decided that it would be a good way to introduce and define myself to the new neighborhood and also to express my appreciation of the efforts of these fine men to keep me and my prospective family safe.

****

I barely noticed when the group decided that they did not want to focus on social activities at this time because I had become increasingly concerned about the welfare of my lady button worker friends. Because my origins within the community are with those who engage in physical labor for a living, I have maintained a considerable level of contact with female button workers and relatives of female button workers. I did not speak to Fitch about the concerns of my friends regarding the conditions in the button factories because of his sensitivity over the issue.

I felt his increasing annoyance over the local button company lock-out and strike. He thought that the owners were doing everything that they could to accommodate their workers. He believed that an employer had the right to set whatever salary and working conditions that he wants and that, if the employee did not like the work setting, he should quit and find work elsewhere. He spoke of the levels of investment and risks that are taken on by a businessman in the regular course of business and the lack of understanding that the workers have of that.

Fitch has mentioned the coffee pot that one of the owners had installed in his factory as a concrete sign of their positive intent. I am not certain that he fully comprehended the extent of women and women's issues involved in the conflict. I hope that he does not speak out loudly in the community about his view of this issue. It could be considered a bit of an insult to the workers to imply that all of their safety, health and fairness concerns should be met by the provision of a coffee pot and a cafeteria.

I am aware through communication with my contacts that all of the work in the button factories is segregated with the women performing different tasks in separate areas. My button polisher friends told me how the polishers were mostly girls of 14 to 15 years old who arranged the buttons on a moving belt to be smoothed by the machinery. These polishing machines had no exhaust tubes and the workers spent their days coughing and choking their way through a thick atmosphere of unfiltered shell dust. On top of that the drilling and pressing machines had no guards or protections and frequently gashed or cut off workers' fingers. Despite a state law prohibiting women from cleaning machines in motion, my women friends in the button factories were required to do so and often a fine was deducted from wages if the machine was not properly cleaned. (Annals of Iowa, Volume 46, Issue 4 (spring 1982) The Muscatine Button Workers' Strike of 1911-12, Kate Rousmaniere, pgs 243-262)

A major cause of concern was the piece work system. The woman, as well as many of the men, were paid according to the number of pieces or buttons that they produced. As you can imagine, the counting or weighing of buttons therefore became a major source of concern. My friends felt that there were methods put in place that prevented the correct counting of their pieces of production. Their suspicions were heightened by the fact that they were not allowed to view the weighing. It was reported to me that some factories actually held noon religious services for the workers when the management supposedly 'counted' the buttons. (Annals of Iowa, Volume 46, Issue 4 (spring 1982) The Muscatine Button Workers' Strike of 1911-12, Kate Rousmaniere, pgs 243-262)

This piece work system also caused the women to work faster and faster in order to make the same amount of money due to the fact that the owners were in the habit of regularly raising the piece rate. Because of the increased need for speed, my friends are often forced to work beyond the point where they feel they can perform the task competently. The manufacturers claimed that of every 168 buttons made, 24 would be imperfect. The workers were not paid for the labor and time of making the extra 24 buttons therefore many of the women felt a need to take cards to their homes after spending full days in the factories, to continue sewing buttons on cards in order to make enough money to care for their families. Thus the need to make enough money for survival not only took them away from their children for the entire day, but also stole away any time that they might spend with them in the evening. (Annals of Iowa, Volume 46, Issue 4 (spring 1982) The Muscatine Button Workers' Strike of 1911-12, Kate Rousmaniere, pgs 243-262)

When some of my friends and their sympathizers attempted to stage a demonstration many were badly clubbed. Several of my ladies were arrested and charged for using vile and improper language and 2 were arrested for refusing to move when told to do so. (The Muscatine Journal, October 27, 1911, pg 2, "Police Clash With Crowds Near M'Kee & Bliven Button Plant")

Of course my friends fought back and threw shells, rocks and bricks at the officers because of their belief that the police were acting unlawfully and that they, as American citizens, had the right to assemble and peaceably demonstrate in their own home community.

These women told me about a parade that they had helped organize for the purpose of ensuring that the community was aware of their issues. They felt certain that they would have broad support from the community when they knew of the treatment of their mothers, wives and sisters. The roots of this state have primarily been in agriculture and farm women are known to work in the often harsh climate, under the most difficult conditions, right alongside their husbands in the fields and barns. Their efforts have traditionally been appreciated and respected and it was believed that maltreatment at the hands of button factory owners would not be tolerated by the community.

At the urging of my friends and without the knowledge of Fitch, I took the streetcar downtown to see the union parade that took place on the 10th of April. I was not prepared for all that I observed that day. In fact my education began prior to the beginning of the procession.

Before I arrived at the parade route I noticed that a large crowd of people had gathered around the Commercial Hotel where it is believed that the police force that has been hired from outside of the state is housed. As I approached the throng, I heard it announced that Rosie Dietrich, a little girl who was struck by one of these hired police at a conflict at a local plant, was dying. The crowd's level of resentment about the presence and behavior of this hired police force reached a high level and threats began to be shouted out and stones were thrown, several of which smashed through the windows of the hotel.

The county attorney, at great risk to himself, climbed up on the steps of the building and addressed the crowd. He said that the special officers had left the area and were not in the hotel at all. He announced that martial law had been declared and that the police powers had been taken from the special officers. He begged the crowd to disperse. (The Muscatine Journal, April 14, 1911, pg 2, "ANGRY CROWD THREATENS IMPORTED SPECIAL POLICE")

I, of course, immediately left the area and was drawn to the enormous throng that had gathered on the street to watch the parade. The parade had begun and was led by important union men, followed by a band. The main body of the parade was made up of union representatives and members, including many of my lady friends. They marched by carrying signs which said, "What girl ever got a fair deal in a button factory?" There were several hundred girls in the procession and their presence was the occasion for the greatest cheering. (The Muscatine Journal, April 14, 1911, pg 2, "ANGRY CROWD THREATENS IMPORTED SPECIAL POLICE")

One of them waved at me and yelled above the crowd, "Follow us to Hare's Hall, Elsie, where the meeting of the evening is to be held." I scurried along beside the group and was amazed to observe that as the head of the parade reached the front of the meeting hall, the procession halted and then parted to form lines on either side of the street. While the girl workers marched through the gang of brother workmen into the hall the men paid tribute to them by baring their heads and greeting them with cheers.

I was surprised at the support that my friends had from the male union members. These events increased my understanding of what was happening in the community.

Why would the male workers have reacted in such a way if they felt that the ladies were being treated fairly by the owners? Their emotions clearly indicate that they are of the opinion that the women are acting in a heroic fashion by continuing to work in the industry.

The level of support that I observed from the cheering crowds causes me to reach the conclusion that there is wide community support for the workers. I wonder if Fitch is aware of this. Does he comprehend that his support of the owners might cause this segment of the public to lower their opinion of him and could affect his business?

I know how he would respond if I mentioned this to him. He would say, "Elsie, I must do what I know is the right thing no matter how the business is affected. If those ladies feel that they are being treated unfairly they should stay home and take care of their children. Nobody is forcing them to work in the button industry."

He is right, of course but for many mothers working is not perceived as a choice. We are dependent on the men in our lives to feed us and care for us and our children. Fitch does not comprehend how many men there are in the world that are incapable or unwilling to work. Many men do not think and behave as he does.

There is no point in discussing these issues with him at much length. He does not understand how it is to be needy because he has never had the experience. He doesn't know what a mother will do when her children are hungry and cold. He cannot comprehend the anxiety caused by having the welfare of her young ones totally dependent on the positive intentions and behaviors of the males in her life. I do.

George Volger

The number of people that patronized Swan Jewelry in order to visit with me increased regularly throughout my employment. Although I have been absent periodically due to traveling throughout the country with the Muscatine Basketball team, any economic cost for Mr. Swan due to my absences have certainly been compensated by the people that come in to visit upon my return. There were often groups of men gathered around to discuss the strategy of the last ball game or the next and at such times he was in the back polishing rings or repairing watches while I was up front socializing with the public. After a while, I could sense that this situation was annoying Mr. Swan.

Cornelius suggested that I do something to alter the circumstances. He said that the state of affairs was rightly anger provoking to Mr. Swan but that he was too much of a gentleman to inform me of his level of annoyance. Cornelius emphasized that, as a man with intimate experience with anger issues, he recognized the dilemma that this was creating for his uncle.

I agreed that the circumstances were not flattering to Mr. Swan but I could not figure out how to handle this situation. If I was not friendly and communicative with the visitors of the store, I would run the risk of offending potential customers and they might stop patronizing the establishment. I also did not know how to discuss this with Mr. Swan. What could I say? "I am sorry that people like me more than they like you, Mr. Swan. I am sorry that I have been a star athlete with whom people want to discuss the sports scene." I could think of no polite way to approach the subject.

It did not help the situation when Elsie Swan got into the practice of bringing pastries to the store once or twice a week. Although she indicated that she was bringing them to share with all who entered the building, I sensed that her underlying motivation was to visit with me. Elsie and I shared a lot of social and political views and she seemed to identify me as an anchor in her upper crust life.

I recall one day in particular, when she came rushing into the store, clutching a rather dirty little stone that she had found on the riverbank. Mr. Swan examined the stone and declared it to be a Lake Superior agate and indicated to Elsie that it was of little value. Her disappointment was palpable. Without any thought, I told her to give it to me. I sliced it and polished it, and secured it in a gold setting that I attached to a gold chain. She accepted it graciously upon its completion.

Although I knew that this offended Mr. Swan, I could not refrain from intervening. As usual, he was technically correct about the situation but had little comprehension of the emotion involved. The value of the stone to Elsie had nothing to do with its classification as a precious or semi-precious stone. The fact of the matter was that the stone had value to Elsie because she herself found it along the river and she saw beauty within it. If the man does not pay more attention to her emotional needs, he will not be able to sustain the marriage.

****

I had hoped that the relationship between Mr. Swan and myself would improve when Cornelius opened his own jewelry business about a block up the street. Since

Cornelius had experienced some success in managing his anxiety it seemed likely that this venture would prove successful. In addition, this would result in Mr. Swan no longer having Cornelius to depend upon and that he would need to lean more on me. It seemed probable that this would increase our communication and understanding of each other. Although I tried my best to enhance our relationship, improvement did not happen and tension continued to increase between Mr. Swan and myself.

It was clear after a few years, that Cornelius was not having the necessary level of success in his new business venture and it was suggested that I take over his store while he moved back to Mr. Swan's store to replace me. I was excited about the notion. It was apparent to me that I could succeed in operating my own business and that I would prosper in the level of freedom that being my own boss would provide. My competitive spirit is quite developed. Thus in May of 1911, I bought Cornelius' fixtures and began my own operation in his location. (The Muscatine Journal, May 11, 1911, pg 4, "Muscatine Young Man in Business")

The grand opening was quite successful. Crowds of people came into my store and although there was a bit of decline afterwards, there continued to be enough traffic to allow me to purchase current and beautiful stock. I had been concerned while working at Swan's that much of the stock had sat on the shelves for several years. I felt that I could impress his customers with stock of the latest designs and styles.

The quantity of people visiting my business also increased, I believe, by the passions aroused by the pearl button lock-out. Most of my friends were my age and many were employed by the button industry or sympathized with the workers' plight. As tensions increased, my store became the hub of information. The population poured in to hear what was happening among the workers, how the community was responding and what was planned for the future.

Tensions seemed to begin with the formation of the Button Workers Protective Union on October 18th, 1910. The union was formed to protect those working in the button industry from the injustices that have been inflicted upon them for years by their employers. On Feb, 25th, 1911, the button manufacturers locked the doors of their factories against their workers and told them that they could get their jobs back only if they destroyed their union cards. (The Muscatine Journal, August 31, 1911, pg 2, "CONDEMN CARROLL IN RESOLUTIONS")

The union responded in a predictable fashion. They said that they would under the condition that there be a union shop granted by the owners and total recognition of the Button Workers Protective Union. Since accurate counting of production was a central concern to the workers they focused their needs upon the standardization and transparency of the button weighing and counting methods.

My worker friends have told me that there has been a 25 to 50 percent decrease in wages during the past few months although they have continued to work at the same speed. When confronted about this situation the owners asserted that the shrinkage was due to the irregularity of work completed because of the lack of concentration and focus on their tasks. They said that the men had focused on unionization and were gathering in groups during the working hours talking and arguing, while their machines were left unattended and nonproductive, just rattling along on their own, burning energy and producing nothing.

The manufacturers caused the sheriff to hire thugs from Chicago and St. Louis to police the streets and supported him in his eventual proclamation of

Military Law. It was indicated that the forming of crowds was prohibited and that people will not be allowed to congregate on the streets, and will be kept moving. He notified the citizens to keep away and stated that if they join any crowds and get hurt it will be their own fault and that he could not be responsible for them.

After public outrage caused the hired thugs to be disbanded and replaced by National Guard troops, the union encouraged the workers to remain peaceful and to devote their time to urging workers to continue the work stoppage until a reasonable agreement could be reached between management and the union. They requested that every union member visit all non-union workers in their homes and ask them to refrain from working.

****

I was anxious and excited about the planned union parade which I watched from the street in front of my store. I expected it to be rather large because I believed that the workers had the support of the community but I was actually overwhelmed by the enormity of the gathering. Many of them waved at me and cheered as they passed on the street.

"More than fifteen hundred people marched through the downtown district of the city, along streets indented with deep rows of spectators. The procession was about nine blocks long and required more than fifteen minutes to pass a given point. As the members of the various labor bodies marched along the crowded thoroughfares, the sympathizers with the button workers and the supporters of the unionists' cause applauded mightily and frequent cheering was heard. The presence of the great crowd and the cheers and applause formed tributes to unionism. (The Muscatine Journal, April 14, 1911, pg 2, "ANGRY CROWD THREATENS IMPORTED SPECIAL POLICE")

I went up to Elsie Swan who was standing by the curb among a group of men, and seemed to be mesmerized by the spectacle. "Hi, Elsie," I said. "Pretty remarkable, isn't it?"

"Oh my word, George, I never thought that my worker friends had this level of support in the community."

"Where is your husband?" I asked.

"I am sure that he is busy with customers in his store," she responded. "He certainly doesn't have the time to stand out in the middle of the street and watch a parade."

67

Although I did not react to her criticism, it did cross my mind that, if I was Fitch Swan, I would leave my store and spend my time with her rather than have her hanging around groups of men. I am fond of Elsie, but it is clear that she often does not have a good perception of her effect on young men. It is uncommon for the wife of a businessman to spend time standing on the street corner, conversing with the opposite sex, in our community. People might certainly get the wrong impression.

The labor conflict continued until the ministerial association became involved. They drafted a resolution that both parties submit their differences to an impartial board of arbitration. The workers agreed to this resolution but the owners turned it down. The button company workers refused to recognize the union and to meet with union members. The officers of the manufacturers' association eventually stated that they planned to move away their machines until so few remain that they have three men for one job in Muscatine. The end of this labor war finally concluded with an agreement between the manufacturers and workers on May 2nd.

Chapter 3: 1912 and 1913
Fitch

It was clear to Cornelius following the rather dismal holiday season that my business had not recovered from the Volger store competition as rapidly as expected and he once again, approached the notion of opening his own store. He seemed to think that my business would have more funds available if I did not have to pay his salary. I attempted to convince him that this was an insufficiently thought-out response to a complex situation. Another jewelry store in the area would not serve as a solution. Cornelius had made up his mind, however, and had been searching potential properties. He found a suitable space on the corner about a block away and opened in February. (The Muscatine Journal, February 5, 1912, pg 8, Cadle Store Ad)

After Cornelius left, I spent a lot of time poring over my books. I reduced expenses for the business to the lowest level it could tolerate and still succeed. I looked through my piles of sales brochures and magazines and identified affordable merchandise that would be new to the community and might draw interest. There were silver filled spoons, knives and forks in sterling silver patterns available at half the cost of sterling. Because these items were plated instead of a more pure form of silver, they cost me less to stock and I could also sell them for a lower price than the silverware sold in other stores. I thought they were a certain winner and would bring in more customers. My optimism began to rise as there was an encouraging but slight uptick in traffic and sales.

****

I arrived home one evening to find Elsie sitting at the kitchen table with papers spread out before her. She was buzzing with excitement, her cheeks bright red and her curly hair flying in all directions. "What are you up to, Elsie?" I asked.

Her eyes sparkled as she said, "I am planning a big party, Fitch. It is just what we need to welcome the season of winter with our friends. I have always wanted to plan a Halloween Party. Just think of it... Jack-o-lanterns, witches, candied apples. There is so much possibility with Halloween!"

"Oh my, Elsie. How many people are you planning to invite? Perhaps we could just have an intimate get-together. You will soon be decorating the house for Thanksgiving and then Christmas. Do you really think you need to decorate for Halloween too?"

"I know you are aware, Fitch, that a person cannot be married to the premier creator of pieces of art in the community and not reflect that beauty in her own home. People expect to come into your residence and observe how an artist lives. They would be so disappointed to be invited here and find a few of their neighbors sitting in a dimly lit, colorless interior. We cannot do that in this community. It is your reputation, your image we must always consider. We shall invite all of our friends and neighbors and will have beautiful decorations and the most memorable food. We are known for that, Fitch. That is who we are."

The previous optimism and hope that I had experienced began to deflate. *I don't know how we can keep this up,* I thought. *Maybe I should tell her that we just can't afford to do this right now.* The problem is that she is right. This is our image in the community... this is our brand. If we stop having parties people will suspect that there are economic problems and she is so alive and so happy when she is planning parties.

I continued to have a strong belief in the future of the retail conditions. Muscatine was experiencing economic success. It promised a future of opulence and wealth. I must not give the impression to the community that I have changed that view. How ludicrous it seemed that I am sinking while all other aspects of the community are rising. Surely I could pull myself out of this situation? This is not permanent.

In addition, would Elsie want to stay with me if she knew of the scope of our economic problems? Would she leave me? I feel quite certain that she would stay and would continue to love me but I don't want to take the chance. I couldn't endure losing Elsie along with everything else.

I said nothing to Elsie about the state of our business and we had a Halloween party that surpassed any our little town has ever seen in our home at Sheltering Oaks.

****

April is a tough time in Iowa. Following the endless silence of winter, the world begins to come alive in starts and stops. Periods of ice and snow are followed with the songs of robins and hesitant little tentacles of green reaching through the soil. Once the joy of the promise of life is experienced, the sky darkens, snow begins to fall and all hope shrivels along with the greenery. It doesn't take long to learn to make the most out of any comfortable day in April.

Thus after Elsie, Aunt Anna and I had dinner one lovely evening in April, we took a stroll through Weed Park. There was a warm breeze from the south and we noticed the beginning swelling of small leaf buds on the trees. As we stood by the Indian mounds and watched the Mississippi snake off into the distance, Elsie said, "Fitch, I have something to tell you but I don't want you to get upset."

"What is it, Elsie?"

"While I was in the Kautz Bakery last week, Mr. Kautz asked me if I had heard that George is closing his present store and opening one on the same block as yours, just a few stores away. I pretended that we were well aware of it and were in favor of the plan.

I didn't want him to think that George had tricked us."

"Oh my God, Elsie. Are you serious? Are you sure you heard him correctly?"

"Yes, Fitch. He said that he saw him moving stock into the building."

"This is insane! Surely he cannot think it is a good idea to open a jewelry store just a few feet from my own? It is becoming clear to me that he is not simply attempting to operate a successful business in this community. He is wanting to ruin my business."

As I heard more rumors, I was incredulous. There has been an unsuccessful jewelry store in that location for only 6 months. I watched in astonishment as George moved his stock into this shop that was already outfitted with the very latest type and fashion of fixtures and furniture. (The Muscatine Journal, December 5, 1913, pg 12, "VOLGER'S HOLDING AN ELABORATE OPENING")

I have also heard since then that the egotistical young man has actually handwritten his name in ink on the bottom of one of the cases that were constructed by an artist and craftsman. (The Muscatine Journal, May 23, 2015, pg 1, "New business in Muscatine off to a running start") What a self-promoting little snit. He probably thinks people of the future will assume that he built those cabinets himself.

Following his grand opening a steady stream of people kept going into and coming out of the Volger store. I know that Muscatine people are inquisitive. They will want to inspect anything new that comes along. This trend will not last long. They are loyal people and when they need their watches or jewelry repaired or when they want to buy a stone for their loved ones, they will return to me.

The notion struck me that I need to use "The Old Reliable Jeweler" on my advertising, to remind people of my steadfastness and dependability. It would become my slogan. It would make an advantage of my age. Yes, George was a young athletic popular superstar in the area. But would you really want your watch fixed by him or by "Old reliable" Fitch? I could make use of that.

I also considered a strategy of auction sales. I held an auction in October to 'test-the-waters' of this approach. It was a big auction that included $45,000 in stock including diamonds, watches, clocks, cut glass, jewelry umbrellas, Sterling silverware, etc. I advertised that the stock would be sold for whatever it will bring and that each article sold would be personally guaranteed by myself. I emphasized that ladies were especially invited to attend and that chairs will be provided for them. People flocked to the store for the auction. This approach proved to have real promise for my future.

Weeks went by and the traffic in the Volger store did lessen a little but continued on at a steady pace. I tried to keep my attention on my own business and to ignore the store that was just a few steps from my own. Autumn was coming and with it the customary Christmas business. Retail establishments in downtown Muscatine depend heavily upon sales at the holiday season to keep us in operation. I feel certain that the holidays will reverse our economic trend. It always has in the past and the best predictor of future economic behavior is past economic behavior.

Right before Christmas George installed a fountain and a clock on the street in front of his place of business, along with a street light. (The Muscatine Journal, November 5, 1913, pg 4, "Sanitary Drinking Fountain Arrives") Why in the world would one block on this street require two clocks? How does he figure that his store deserves a street light? He gets a drinking fountain? Of course, these items were installed with much pomp and circumstance. Nobody seemed to notice the elephant in the room: the other clock just a few steps away. This is becoming personal.

Elsie

I know that Fitch is constantly worrying about his business. It seems that no matter how hard he tries, his situation continues to worsen. First there is Cornelius constantly opening and closing shops and then there is George. I am not exactly certain what George is up to. I know that Fitch believes that his relationship with George has become more sinister than that of two business competitors. He is convinced that George is out to destroy him.

That seems a bit over dramatic. I wish that Fitch would walk right up to George and tell him exactly how he feels. I think that he needs to express some of his feelings of anger and betrayal directly to him. It might help to relieve some of the pressure of his built up emotions.

That is not his way of dealing with conflict, however. Fitch believes that it is not productive to express anger towards others and that a man gains strength when he keeps his emotions to himself. He said that a 'real man' does not emote all over the place but that he exerts self control and calmness at all times. He emphasized that women are the emotional sex and that is fine because that is how it is meant to be.

This may be true in his definition of the world, but I am also noticing this negativity having an effect on his behavior. Lately he has become more lethargic and tired. He doesn't joke and laugh like he used to. He does not have the same level of interest in our social engagements and is spending an increasing amount of his free time alone, in Weed Park, sitting on the Indian mounds and staring at the river.

I know what I need to do to fix this situation. Fitch and I must have a child. Actually it is not just for Fitch that a child is needed, but I need a baby in my life also. It is difficult to understand why a pregnancy has not already occurred.

I don't think I would be able to discuss this issue with our common medical doctors but we have an actual woman doctor in this town. In fact it is a family composed of three of the first female doctors in Iowa. Two are located in the same block as Fitch's store and down the Avenue past George Volger's.

The father of the family, Jacob Braunwarth founded a shoe store on the street level floor of the business and sisters Sarah and Emma share a medical office above the store. Another sister, Alice is a pharmacist in the shop next to the shoe store and another sister Anna is also a physician but practices mainly in Chicago. (http://collguides.lib.uiowa.edu/?IWA0863, "Guide to the Sarah Braunwarth papers")

I made an appointment to visit with Dr. Emma. She has the reputation of delivering more $5.00 babies than any other doctor in town. She is also very concerned with the notion of sterility and germs and has been regularly observed wiping off doorknobs and chairs immediately after patients with contagious diseases have left the office. I am a firm believer in the power of germs and I think that she might be the right doctor for me.

The following week, I stole my way past Fitch's and George's front windows, ducked into the building and climbed the stairs to the doctors' reception area. I sat nervously in a waiting room that, to my delight, was full of pregnant women. A nurse escorted me into Dr. Emma's examining room, took my temperature and obtained a basic understanding of the reason for my visit.

Dr. Emma soon knocked on the door, announced herself and walked into the room with a big smile. "Hello, Mrs. Swan, may I call you Elsie?"

"It would be my pleasure, Dr. Braunwarth."

"I understand that you are having concerns about pregnancy, Elsie. Please tell me what is bothering you."

"I have been married to Fitch Swan for five years, we engage regularly in marital relations and yet I have not become pregnant. Fitch is several years older than I and his time for enjoying young children in his life is now. I have tried everything I can think of to facilitate the process but nothing has worked. I am wondering if something is wrong with me physically."

After a complete physical exam, Dr. Emma informed me that there did not appear to be any physical problems. She told me that stress and anxiety often play a part in situations such as mine and advised that I had established an unrealistic pregnancy time-line for myself. It seems that a lot of women do not get pregnant within the first few years of marriage and it does not indicate that they cannot become pregnant in the future. She prescribed a relaxing tonic for me and provided instruction on how I could organize my evening hours in the most calming and peaceful fashion. I felt a sense of relief after the visit with

Dr. Emma. I think she may be correct. Perhaps I have become too tense and distressed about the situation.

As a result of this new understanding, I became energized. I had a plan of action. I was effectively dealing with the problem. I would now busy myself with improving Fitch's mood by engaging him more with his neighbors. I organized the most spectacular Thanksgiving party that this neighborhood has ever seen. I decorated our home in potted pink and white chrysanthemum, and adorned it in a variety of Thanksgiving paraphernalia. A soft glow was provided by carved pumpkins that were placed throughout the home. The evening included dancing and was climaxed with an elegant four course lap supper that was served with guests seated around the fireplace on pillows. I invited members of the Y.W.C.A. and the large social group called "the family" was present.

I had been working for some time on the development of this social organization called the family for the purpose of providing friendship and a sense of having a 'family' for Fitch. We had regular parties and gatherings. Five generations constituted its membership and Fitch was nicknamed "Pa" by the group and I was called "Mother". (The Muscatine Journal, November 1, 1912, pg 5, ""The Family" In Revel at "Sheltering Oaks" Thursday") Fitch told me that it was no small thing that I had found such a creative way to involve ourselves with so many neighbors. He said, "There is nothing more important than the love that family and friends add to my life."

George

My father, George Volger Sr. finally gave up the fight, closed his saloon and retired this year. I have mixed feelings about it since much of my childhood was spent assisting my father in various ways in the saloon business. It has provided me with an education that most young men do not have. I know how to greet people and make them feel welcome. I have learned how to ask exactly the right question and also when to just shut up and listen. I am skilled at stopping arguments and quieting people down. A lot of my education in social interaction was obtained by watching my father and his bartenders deal with a variety of people in a variety of situations.

Perhaps the most unusual situation that I observed my father handle was the visit from Carrie Nation, a leader of the temperance movement. She happened to decide to grace Muscatine and my father's saloon with her presence in 1901, which was the same year that I became a clerk at Swan's store. Her manager, A.C. Rankin, announced that Carrie would visit this city for the purpose of delivering a temperance lecture under the auspices of the Young People's Christian Temperance union. (The Muscatine Journal, February 9, 1901, pg 7, "More About Mrs. Nation")

We families with saloons expected the worse when we heard of Mrs. Nation's rampage throughout Kansas. It was said that she began her crusade against the Topeka saloons at six o'clock in the morning accompanied by nine members of the hatchet brigade of her "home defenders". After she hatcheted, smashed and caused $2,000 worth of damage at one saloon, a porter grabbed a revolver from the bar and fired two shots at her as she headed toward a large plate glass mirror with her hatchet upraised. Although he missed, she was struck in the face with the flat side of the hatchet when scuffling with the proprietor who was attempting to disarm her. She was arrested and charged with malicious destruction. (The Muscatine Journal, February 5, 1901, pg 1, "Shots Fired at Mrs. Nation")

Stopping Nation from visiting the saloons of Muscatine or attempting to gain her understanding of the cultural heritage that is tied to alcohol in this area was not even a possibility to consider. She believed that she had a mission from God and that God infused her with the strength and power to complete her tasks. God entered her soul and allowed her to defeat Satan disguised in the form of saloon keepers. She actually said that, "She felt invincible. Her strength was that of a giant. God was certainly standing by her. She smashed five saloons with rocks before she ever lifted a hatchet".

The Muscatine saloon keepers were uncertain of what to expect from Mrs. Nation. My father told the newspaper reporter that, "If she comes to my saloon, I will turn the hose on her."

L.C. Lang, proprietor of the German Village, said, "I will kick her out if she comes here. I am German and keep a clean saloon with no wine rooms or disreputable people about and she has no right to come here and bother me."

Adam Von Dresky, proprietor of the saloon at the corner of Sycamore and First streets echoed the sentiments of many Muscatine saloon owners when he said, "I expect her to visit my place the first one and make a general clean out. I would not harm her but I would try and protect my property." (The Muscatine Journal, February 8, 1901, pg 1, "Muscatine Saloon Keepers In Fear of Mrs. Nation")

****

As Mrs. Nation's train moved across the state, my father and his fellow saloon keepers waited anxiously for news of her activities. They were informed that when she stepped out on the train car platform to make a statement to the assembled crowd at Iowa City she said, "Go thou and do likewise if you intend to defend yourself and do it now, I am working in the cause of God and his work I will accomplish. This is a college town and I advise you young men to defend your precious lives by fighting the saloon." (The Muscatine Journal, February 11, 1901, pg 1, "Far Famed Smasher Is In Muscatine")

She was greeted by a large cheering crowd as the train approached West Liberty. She stepped down from the train and spoke to the enthusiastic assembly. "Young men," she said, "go to smashing at once and get a reputation. You are only little pigs, but can easily save some of the many big hogs who are killing themselves with liquor. I will not do hatchet smashing in Muscatine, but will give full directions as how to carry on the smashing." A man in the crowd shouted out that there had not been a saloon in West Liberty for forty years. Carrie raised her voice in praise to the Lord. (The Muscatine Journal, February 11, 1901, pg 1, "Far Famed Smasher Is In Muscatine")

Once again, the train began to move and Carrie climbed aboard and rode in the car until it arrived at Wilton. The president of the German college met her at the depot and induced her to make a short speech, which was received with prolonged cheers by the large company of students and others who had assembled to meet her. (The Muscatine Journal, February 11, 1901, pg 1, "Far Famed Smasher Is In Muscatine")

As the train approached Muscatine, Carrie held her head out of the window on the river side and waved her hand at the crowd two blocks before the depot was reached. "Cheers greeted her all along the way as the train steamed past the factories which line the route into the city and many boarded the moving car to shake hands with her. Once or twice she reached down and shook hands with men as the train moved along. She was met at the depot by an enthusiastic crowd of 2,000 people, who pushed and shoved each other like a stampede among cattle in their efforts to get a glimpse of her. When the train finally stopped she viewed the crowd with a smiling countenance. Some little boys pushed their way to the front and she said, "Ah, there are some little smashers. The saloons have got to go now, boys; we'll smash them back to hell where they came from won't we?" (The Muscatine Journal, February 11, 1901, pg 1, "Far Famed Smasher Is In Muscatine")

That evening, my father and I attended her speech at the Grand. She aroused the passions of the crowd. She told the audience that she had spent twenty days in jail, had been rawhided, broom sticked, and had received a black eye in a saloon and had been struck, all without the slightest impulse to defend herself. She said that she believed that there would not be a saloon left in the country within a year's time and that her efforts would then be transferred to drive saloons out of other lands. She claimed to receive from 150 to 200 letters a day part of which say that she should come for God's sake and clean out the saloons and a few saying that if she came she would never leave, for they had her grave already dug and they would bury her with her boots on. (The Muscatine Journal, February 12, 1901, pg 4, "Company Breaks Up")

When we arrived home after the speech, my father sat down at the kitchen table with me and had a drink. "What did you think of her, Dad?" I asked.

"She makes me want to have a drink," dad replied. "There is no reasoning with somebody like that."

"What do you think she will do tomorrow?"

"I have no idea what she will do," he said. "She thinks that whatever pops into her head at any minute is an order from God, so there is no way to predict what her behavior will be. All of us saloon owners have met and have decided that our best strategy is to be as calm and pleasant as we possibly can so that we do not rile up her emotions. Of course, we can't stand by while she destroys our property but we will try to be like sponges and soak up her insults and anger and give her no reason to feel a need to prolong her visit."

The following morning, Carrie began her tour of Muscatine "sampling rooms". She left the hotel at seven o clock accompanied by the city marshal, deputy marshal and a delegation of reporters and visited several leading saloons of the city, and in each one she provided a great deal of advice to the proprietor or bartender who was in charge. To her surprise, she was met with a smile by most of the saloon men.

The Well was the first saloon entered and she spoke directly to proprietor Crippen. "I want to tell you that I come as a friend and ask you why you are running this place?" Crippen informed her that the business was being carried on with the sole purpose of making money. Carrie replied, "Why do you not murder or commit robbery to get money? It is far better to do that than to run such a criminal making shop as this. I say, get out of business." (The Muscatine Journal, February 12, 1901, pg 4, "Company Breaks Up")

At Wier's saloon, Carrie commented on the number of Indian relics and made a short temperance talk. She then went to the Grand Annex and made another talk stating that "she hated the murder shops and hell dives of the city, but loved the bartender and proprietor for no matter how wicked they might be she could discern a little good within them". (The Muscatine Journal, February 12, 1901, pg 4, "Company Breaks Up")

Things went rather well until she visited the Von Dresky's saloon. Upon entering the place and seeing the very fine interior decorations she became distressed at the opulence and said, "I see naked babies, women crying for help and men in hell in all these fine decorations." Her eyes then fell upon a debasing picture hung on the wall and she shouted with vehemence, "I tell you to take that picture down. I order that you take it down. That is your mother's form. Would you have your mother there?" She was told that it was simply a work of high art that might be seen in the best of homes and she answered, "Oh no. It is not high art. I order you to take it down. Don't let me see that here tonight. Oh. The hungry children that built this palace. I can see the blood of their veins being sucked away. Blood, blood, blood." Another picture came within range of her eyes as she was about to leave and speaking in sharp terms to the bartender, she ordered it removed and left." (The Muscatine Journal, February 12, 1901, pg 4, "Company Breaks Up")

She next stopped at my dad's saloon. We had runners following her around and running back to the bar to inform us of her progress. As she was arriving, I said to my father, "Remember, Dad, keep her calm. Try to not get angry no matter what she says. If we get riled up she gets riled up. It sounds like the owners have been successful with the strategy so far."

Dad and I could hear her coming as crowds of people followed her along the street. She suddenly burst into the room and demanded to talk to the proprietor. My father stepped forward, smiled and introduced himself. She made no effort to engage in friendly conversation with him. In her 'loud-for-public-impact' voice she asserted that it was "far better for my father to be a murderer or robber than to run such a place and ruin character, reputation and even kill, besides constantly throwing souls to the devil". (The Muscatine Journal, February 12, 1901, pg 4, "Company Breaks Up")

Dad put on his most saddened face, nodded his head up and down and sighed. Then she made the statement that quieted the whole room. "She said that she could pity him somewhat because he was a German, and was not educated on the temperance question as is the average American". (The Muscatine Journal, February 12, 1901, pg 4, "Company Breaks Up") Although Dad's face turned bright red he, once again, sighed and nodded his head. Great relief was experienced by all when she walked out of the door and Dad ordered a round of free drinks for everyone.

After she left our saloon she went on to several others in the community. She was, once again, shocked by what she considered to be vulgar pictures when she entered the commercial Annex. She exclaimed that they were the worst pictures that she had ever seen in all of her life. She ordered that they be removed and stated that she would leave a delegation of women in this city that would visit the place and see if her orders were complied with. (The Muscatine Journal, February 12, 1901, pg 4, "Company Breaks Up")

She then took fruit to the 'innocent', as she termed the men in the county jail and, upon their request, prayed for them. When she was at the depot to catch the train that would transport her to Chicago, several saloonkeepers were waiting for her. One became engaged in a heated discussion about the saloon question with her and asked if she would not now take a little advice from him since he had already listened to so much from her. She replied that she had never yet received any good advice from the devil. (The Muscatine Journal, February 12, 1901, pg 4, "Company Breaks Up")

As we were all celebrating the departure of Mrs. Nation, we learned that she had given out a letter addressed to saloonkeepers' wives. At the end of the day we brought one such letter home for my mother. It read, "To Wives of Saloonkeepers: My Darling Sisters: My heart goes out to you and I intend to help you and your precious lambs. I freely give you a share of the money I take in so that you need not fear that you will suffer. I shall devote myself to seeing that you have good homes and no longer have the vicious enemy within that destroys the love of home and you. If there is a wife of any saloonkeeper who is in want because the business of selling rum is smashed, write me and I will see so far as possible that you are instantly relieved. No longer will you eat the bread of the hungry and wear the clothes of the naked. No longer shall you live by killing others. Let me hear from you and accept the devotion of a sister." (The Muscatine Journal, February 12, 1901, pg 4, "Company Breaks Up")

"Well, that's a relief," said my mother. "I no longer need to worry about my future because Carrie Nation will take care of me. I think I will just take off my 'clothes of the naked' and go to bed and I suggest that you two do the same. It has been a long and trying day."

"I will drink to that," replied my father.

****

Iowa is no state in which to run a saloon, having had a history of prohibition since its territorial days. Laws have been proposed, passed and appealed on such issues as outlawing any liquor except for homemade liquor, outlawing liquor of any kind, requiring signatures of consenting members of a community to open a bar, outlawing alcohol at sports games, prohibiting any theatrical or operatic performance, athletic exhibition or concert of any description which occurs on a Sunday to sell alcohol. (http://www.dsaiowa.com/History.htm "The Prohibition Years")

In addition, Muscatine had a peculiar atmosphere all of its own. The Mulct Law was passed by the Iowa legislature and required that a prospective saloon owner circulate a petition in order to obtain a certain number of signatures approving his operating a saloon. The petition needed to be filed with the county for approval. Any citizen could file a civil case against a saloon owner thought to be violating the conditions of the act and get injunctive relief closing the saloon as a nuisance or setting conditions of its continued operation. (http://www.dsaiowa.com/History.htm "The Prohibition Years")

The National German American Alliance was formed a few years ago to promote and preserve German culture in America. It promoted German language instruction in schools, advocated the foundation of educational societies including the German American Historical Society and the publication of histories and journals to demonstrate the role German Americans had played in the development of the United States. The resolutions passed condemned prohibition and endorsed, instead, a strict regulation of the liquor traffic.

The struggle of this organization is a broad struggle, which has met with limited success. It has given my father a reason to hope over the years, but the ongoing reality of the situation is, in my view, really quite hopeless. Its philosophy is not acceptable to many American people, who have a strong belief in assimilation. It is a desire for all people to jump into a big American soup pot and melt into one consistent broth.

The National German Alliance sought to resist the assimilation of Germans in America, which sounds like an astonishing statement. What the German people mean by this is that we do not want to disappear. We do not want to become identical with the English. We are proud of our origins and celebrate our culture.

There will always be German foods cooking in my home. My family will always sing our Christmas carols in German. Many of us will talk with an accent even when we make our best efforts to speak English and, of course, our exquisite melodies will always exist within our souls. There are many things in our histories that we will preserve and will bequeath to our children.

At the same time we are good Americans and believe in the freedoms that this country provides. We will join with the English and the Irish and all other Americans to fight for the values that we share and, at the same time, we will honor the traditions of each other. Beer has been part of our cultural heritage and celebrations since our beginnings. We do not view its consumption as anti-American or anti-God. It has been difficult for my father and mother to comprehend the emotions behind this 'battle'. It seems to them that the sentiment is contrary to their culture and identity.

The saloons of the community had never operated under a petition of consent as required by the Mulct Law and on January 1st of 1908, for the first time in history, with the exception of a brief period in 1893, the saloon doors were locked. Petitions were filed with the Board of Supervisors and were declared insufficient. Once declared insufficient, another petition could not be legally filed until the expiration date of one year from the date of the last petition submitted. (The Muscatine Journal, December 16, 1909, pg 45, "Muscatine the little dry town on the bend", www.usaiowa.com/images/Prohibition.pdf) What a clever way to destroy an industry.

How could a person operate a business that is under constant threat of being closed down? Our family wondered what was going on in reality. Was this simply an anti-German effort or was it a big business effort aimed at the workers? It was thought that most of the patrons of the saloons were working people. Did the business owners think that they would get more consistent labor out of their employees if they did not gather at bars? Were they concerned that union conspiring occurred in these long evenings?

My father thought that this was aimed against the German immigrant population. He viewed it as an anti-German movement. Large numbers of us German people came to the United States in the 1850's as a result of the failed struggle for liberty in Germany in 1848-1850. Many have settled in this area. Alcohol is an integral part of our German culture and many of us like to have our celebrations or 'fests' on Sundays and to include beer. Both the beer consumption and the celebrations on Sunday seem to scandalize the non-German Protestants. (http://www.dsaiowa.com/History.htm "The Prohibition Years") They appear to see Sunday as a religious time of rest, not of partying. We don't care if they rest on Sunday but we find it hard to understand how they feel that they can dictate that behavior to our population.

Meanwhile Dad and the other saloon owners have modified their businesses to become restaurants or cafes when necessary with the plan to switch back to saloons if it ever becomes possible again. Dad and the other proprietors have also found a source of unique and supposedly non-alcoholic beverages. In Davenport, Burlington and Keokuk instead of ordering 'beer' a customer would order 'mum'. In neighboring Clinton the saloons served 'hopinine.' Although these were sold as 'non alcoholic beverages' customers were observed staggering out of the establishments, on occasion, after consumption of the liquid. (http://www.dsaiowa.com/History.htm "The Prohibition Years")

****

83

I want my father and mother out of this mess. My parents are simply operating a business for profit. They enjoy the company of others and have appreciated the opportunity to provide a comfortable gathering place for social interaction. People came to the bar to meet with friends, to relax and to decompress from their daily stress. Demonizing saloon owners has been too common and my parents are not the spawn of Satan. I think my father and mother have tolerated enough. I want for them to have some years to relax and enjoy life. They deserve to experience rewards for a lifetime of hard work. They will now have enough leisure time to spend some time at my new store.

Volger Store

My decision to open a jewelry store at a new location is partially a result of my father's retirement. A jewelry store on the block of Fitch Swan's store became available and I purchased the stock, lease, fixtures and entire establishment. (The Muscatine Journal, May 6, 1913, pg 9, "GEO. H. VOLGER BUYS NEW JEWELRY STORE") The store had only been in business for six months so I got a great deal on brand new stock and fixtures. Not only that, but the location is 110 East Second Street and is next to the street car and interurban waiting rooms (The Muscatine Journal, May 15, 1913, pg 5, Volger Ad) which is, in my view, a prime location for attracting the interest of possible customers. I was profiting at my old location but the potential profit at this new spot is so good that I could not pass up the opportunity.

Mom and Dad will most likely transition into retirement easier if they have my new store to focus upon. I will ask them to assist with the move and the business plan. This will finally give my father an unconstrained opportunity to develop and implement marketing strategies without the constant worry of the law. It is strange but true that an honest businessman will undergo a very different experience in operating a jewelry store rather than a saloon.

I assume that Fitch Swan will understand this move and is mature enough to comprehend the nature of business. Business is a competitive sport and is very similar to the sports in which I engage. You play the game to win the game. A good player keeps his eye on the goal. Individual competitors are, in themselves, irrelevant. It is the attainment of the goal that matters. If I am to be a successful businessman in this community, I must have the best store at the best location with the best stock and the best management of a great team. There is no point for me to engage in business if I vary from that view.

The competitive nature of business is something that I thoroughly enjoy. As in basketball, it is exhilarating to develop a strategy to outsmart the competition. At times you rejoice when you succeed and you learn rapidly to regroup and attempt another approach when you do not succeed. Fondness or aversion to the competitor is not relevant to the endeavor. It would be wasted time and wasted emotion.

The grand opening of my store occurred in May 1913. Since I planned on stocking only new items at this location, I was able to precede this major sales event with a 'selling out all stock' sale on the old location. Two major community sales attractions occurring one right after the other yielded very good profits. The grand opening included Orchestral Music and treats. The interior with cabinets and fixtures made of the finest mahogany had been decorated with displays of potted plants and cut flowers. The wall cases were backed by heavy plate mirrors and the floor was composed of small stone tiles arranged in a mosaic pattern. (The Muscatine Journal, May 16, 1913, pg 10, "OPENING OF NEW STORE AUSPICIOUS EVENT") Much of the community came to see and enjoy it all. Many of the newly designed jewelry, watches and clocks also attracted buyers.

Swan's idea to place a large clock on the sidewalk curb outside of his store a couple of years ago was one such brilliant marketing strategy. His creative approach made me chuckle when I first heard of the plan. After much thought, I decided that now is the time to up the ante. I will not only put a clock in front of my store, but it will have my name on it and it will be lighted by a street light and this will occur before Christmas. (The Muscatine Journal, November 5, 1913, pg 4, "Sanitary Drinking Fountain Arrives") The street light is such a unique and appreciated item in this town because of the dark and dreary winter days. The brightness and cheer will certainly attract people to my business during the holidays. In addition to that, I will have a water fountain installed to attract all of those thirsty street car and interurban travelers in our hot and dry summers. This is genius. I am sure that Swan will recognize that. I can hardly wait to see what he will play for the next hand.

Chapter 4: 1914
Fitch

The discovery of vast pools of oil beneath the soil of Texas in 1901 was followed by an explosion of speculation which spread to Oklahoma. There was a great deal of wealth waiting to be pumped out of the earth. Wildcatters came to the Muscatine area reporting that millions in profits were already being made and requested the backing of myself and my friends for the resources to embark on oil drilling ventures. The probability of a major return on an investment, accompanied with the lack of energy required on my part, caused me to invest. This must be divine intervention. It would soon solve the declining profitability that my business was undergoing.

When they saw that I was interested in investment, many of my friends told me of other businesses that they have invested in that promise to be profitable enterprises. Anybody who works in the time consuming and energy demanding field of retail will experience delight at the idea that he could simply send money and yield great profits. Let other people do all of the work. I like that idea.

These prospects increased my confidence in the future and I happily dove into preparation for the holiday season. Elsie came to the store in late autumn and helped me decorate with evergreens and holly berries. She adorned a small Christmas tree in the window with pine cones that were dusted with glitter and red ribbons. She covered empty boxes with gift paper upon which she arranged my jewelry. She placed a small tea pot with some lovely Christmas china tea cups and saucers on my counter near the front. She even drew a large picture of Santa in oils on newsprint that she pinned up to the curtain that led into the back room.

I had to admit that she had some talents but I was a bit disturbed upon noticing that Santa bore a close resemblance to myself. If I gained a few pounds and developed a belly I would be a dead ringer for that Santa. I considered taking it down but decided that such a move would offend Elsie.

Surely this was subconscious on her part? She did not intend to make Santa look like a fat Fitch. I tried to ignore it but found that when friends came into the store they looked at the drawing and commented on how much it looked like me. It was a source of entertainment for many of my customers.

As the season advanced, I did not experience the normal increase in customers. So far the weather was not bad. Perhaps that was slowing things down. I had definite ideas about what weather improved Christmas shopping when I first opened my business. I thought that 'warm and sunny' promised the greatest profits. People would be more willing to come out of their warm homes to shop downtown if it was 'warm and sunny'.

In my first years of business I was surprised to learn that people were in more of a Christmas mood if there was a bit of snow on the ground and that some of my highest traffic days occurred during Muscatine's typical steel gray winter days. It was especially profitable when there were light snow flurries.

I was astonished to find that some people were fond of coming downtown during actual snow storms. The cold wind and driving snow seemed to stimulate them. They would burst through the front door with red cheeks, sparkling eyes, and runny noses. They would gather in groups and chat excitedly about their trials and tribulations in working their way through the 'blizzard'. Then they would bundle up again and push their ways back through the door and out into the vast wasteland. It was interesting entertainment for me but they did not buy anything. They just drank my tea and coffee and ate my cookies.

I have also been informed that the new Iowa Trust and Savings Bank that is coming into town is organizing to go to Cornelius' location. (The Muscatine Journal, January 17, 1914, pg 2, "PLANNED TO ORGANIZE NEW LOCAL BANK SOON") How can he possibly have such bad luck? We have spent many hours together discussing this problem and attempting to find a solution. Cornelius can be certain that I will not let him fail. He has been like a son to me and he and Harriet have helped me through many difficult periods of my life. Now it is my turn to help him. I have not solidified my plan but I have encouraged him to go ahead with an auction before Christmas, in November in hopes of recouping as much money as he can. Surely we will have developed a satisfactory strategy by then?

Once I had invested much of my savings into various ventures, and found that Cornelius may need my financial assistance and that my holiday sales were not progressing as I had hoped, it was made clear to me that Weed Park, next to my home, was in need of new steps and I was asked to provide them. I, of course, agreed. (The Muscatine Journal, May 26, 1914, pg 2, "TO CONSTRUCT STEPS AT WEED PARK SOON") I had just been elected to the board of directors of the Building and Loan and as the Treasurer of the Alert Hose Company. I can't give the community any reason to think that I might have money management issues.

Elsie

Fitch has seemed very depressed since George opened a store just a few steps from his own and, I must say, that neither of us was terribly thrilled to find that George had a son. Of course we wish that he fathers all of the children that he desires to father, but it seems like one more instance of him outperforming us.

I am getting tired of the lack of progress that I am experiencing in the mothering business. I have decided that I will go to speak with the other Braunwarth sister, Doctor Sarah about my lack of success. Perhaps she will have a more productive solution than her sister has had.

I began our conversation by saying, "Dr. Sarah, I cannot understand why I am not becoming pregnant and my concern is increasing that it will never happen for me. I have been working with Dr. Emma and have followed all of her advice and yet, here I am, still not pregnant."

"Tell me about your life, Elsie. What are your dreams and what are your goals?"

"I want to be a mother with many children. I want to maintain a beautiful home full of happy children, with a satisfied husband. I want my family to include many loving members who I can laugh with and cry with. I saw a quote printed on a safe once that said, "Love is a cottage". I have needle pointed that and have hung it in my home. I need to experience that cottage full of loving people. It is something that I have never possessed but have dreamed of all of my life."

"Elsie, you love decorating your home and that indicates an interest and talent in art. The newspapers are always full of events that you have held or have planned. That means that you have some organizational skills. Have you ever considered spending more time in the jewelry store and developing a career interest outside of your home?" she asked.

"Dr. Sarah, I have always been taught that a woman is born to have children and to mother a family. Her body was clearly created for that purpose. I did work before marriage but the role of a woman is to marry and have a family. I cannot think of what I will do if that is not possible."

"Elsie, you need to consider the situation of my sisters and myself. There are three of us sisters who are medical doctors, one who is a pharmacist and one a school principal. None of these are roles that are considered to be traditional for women. These are instead, jobs that we women have wanted to perform; in fact most of us have felt compelled to perform. Can we be mothers and also perform these roles? We quite probably can. Can there be value in the performance of these roles without our being mothers? There most certainly can."

"I am not sure that I would have the support of my family or my community for such a venture. I do not know that I can tolerate the disappointment that others might express in me."

"You can tolerate any criticism, Elsie. It is not as difficult as you think when you are following your own heart."

"Have you or your sisters ever experienced criticism or ridicule for the paths that you have taken?" I asked.

"Oh my, yes," said Dr. Sarah. "I have some documents for you to take home and read that are of criticism that I have received. I want you to read them and think about the words, Elsie and make some decisions about who is in charge of your future. Then you need to come back and we will talk about this some more."

She handed me a packet of papers which I stuffed in my purse and took out the next afternoon when I was seated comfortably on the chaise lounge with a pot of tea. I covered my legs with one of Aunt Anna's afghans and felt properly prepared for a long afternoon of reading.

Dr. Braunwarth had given me an article from the Toledo Medical Compendium in 1891 that contained the following quotes. It was titled, "Should Women Practice Medicine?"

"That women will practice medicine goes without saying, but the advisability of their doing so will long remain open for discussion... the physician knows, as no other can know, that suffering and women are well nigh synonymous terms. From puberty to senility she carries the heavy end of the burden of life. If forbidden the exercise of the function for which she was made, the life-long hunger of her heart can never be satisfied by the husks of business, professional or artistic success. The spinster is an anomaly for which nature makes no provisions. If she marry, and thereby attain motherhood, which is her destiny and crown of rejoicing she must enter this her heaven appointed sphere at the cost of early pain and peril, later pain and danger, and with the prospect of still further pain and jeopardy... Two arguments... present themselves: 1) Can unfortunate, pain afflicted woman ever occupy a sphere of unquestioned usefulness in medicine where physical and mental rigor, fortitude, and endurance are eminently requisite, and the strong must help the weak, help them by virtue of their strength to healthier and stronger states? 2) Can the power of sympathy, operating from the intelligence of affliction and the possible comfort of relief, together with knowledge and discrimination pass from a medical woman to her suffering sex with a probability of extenuating their distress equal as great as would maintain under the fullness of power mentioned in the first proposition?...To our mind, neither the two above deep and dark questions can be answered until the typical woman, that is, the wife and mother shall enter the ranks of medicine. As a rule, she is better employed; and if by chance she be deprived of her natural support, she is too much handicapped by maternity and puberty to begin life in a great profession. Against that large and daily increasing class of involuntary spinsters, which the worthlessness of man and the pinch of poverty have forced to seek support out of the proper sphere of woman no great profession will bar the door. Among these may be found a few who will follow science with masculine force, enthusiasm and success, but the majority ever must be unsexed, discontented, and unsuccessful anomalies, whose only hope for usefulness and happiness is in marriage and its consequences." (The Toledo Medical Compendium, Toledo, Ohio, October 1891, page 366)

Dr. Sarah responded with the following:

"Your October number on page 366 has an article on 'Should Women Practice Medicine? I should answer it by an article on 'Are Not Men Intruders on the Field of Medicine?'

When we take into consideration the millions of cut and sore fingers annually bound up by mothers, the thousands of sore throats, headaches, earaches, and other aches, and the thousand and one ailments of childhood through which others so successfully pilot generation after generation without calling on the Lord of Creation to meddle with the case, we feel that man had usurped the title of physician. It is only when her great anxiety and solicitude for the comfort and welfare of the child prompts the mother to step back, thinking if there is or could anything more be done for the child's comfort and she appeals to a man who pompously steps up and does what? Perhaps something which is not as good as what she has been doing,

In all ages woman has been the real physician of the human race. But it is only lately that she has 'caught on' that a service to be appreciated must be paid for. Out of the unselfish purity of heart, she has ministered night and day to neighbors and relatives and never charged any money for her services. Women, who in county neighborhoods waited on obstetric cases which in number outnumbered many a city practitioner's work in that line, did it for a 'thank you', and that often dispensed with.

But today all that has changed. Our charges are the same as other men charge and Mr. and Mrs. People, you can have your choice at the same price.

You say, 'Women do not do surgery'. Thank stars they did not do some surgery as I have seen. As schoolteachers in days gone by were few and far between, but now are more plentiful, may be, as physicians, our day is coming.

You speak of women's aches and pains. I know many robust Irish and German women who could take you across her knees and spank you in spite of all your resistance, and that at a time when she had a new hopeful kid perhaps but a few days old.

You speak of our 'Mother love hunger,' Mrs. F., one of my neighbors, has a son in the penitentiary in Colorado. They are our best blueblood here. Mrs. K, another neighbor here, has just been presented with a daughter-in-law, recruited from the demi-monde. Don't I wish I had a son?

Statistics prove that one out of every five born in London, die either in the almshouse or in the insane asylum. Don't we women doctors wish we had children? And you personally, if you are my old classmate, Henry H., know it is not for lack of chances that we remain, as most all independent educated women do, unmarried. I cannot strike any crowd of a dozen married women, out of which I can buy a husband for two cents, and they (the women) glad to get rid of them, and as for rent, probably half a dozen would pay the rent to get rid of the men.

Now let us hear no more chestnuts about the health, strength, or ability, either physical or mental, of lady physicians.

Owing to half a dozen interruptions during the writing of this it may read rather jerky."

The editor responded to Sarah's comments with the following:

"Our modern Sarah does not seem to be possessed of a strong mother love hunger, but we believe that ere she reaches the age of the Sarah of old, she will yearn for the blessing that a child will bring to any person, and much more to the female portion of the human race. We remember our schoolmate, Dr. Braunwarth, as a diligent and earnest student, and as a worthy rival of the male portion of the class. We admire the pluck and enthusiastic devotion to medical subjects that she manifested while at school, but we still believe there is a more useful field for woman than is the practice of medicine." (The Toledo Medical Compendium, Toledo, Ohio, October 1891)

I appreciate Dr. Sarah pointing out to me that we are in a time of transition in the medical profession and in the definition of womanhood. I know that before the 1800's there were almost no medical schools, and virtually any enterprising person could practice medicine. You could say you were a doctor, gather a few herbs and begin to practice on people. At that time, obstetrics was actually the domain of women. In fact midwives continue to visit the homes of expectant mothers and deliver their babies.

It is since the 1800's that educational preparation has been required for the practice of medicine. Due to that requirement many young women have been unable to enter the profession. It caused medicine to be defined as a predominantly male field. Dr. Sarah entered medicine in a time of great change both in her profession and in the world at large. I have been told all of my life that women are to work in the home as mothers, wives and housekeepers. I can recall reading in a recent essay that, "women live in a distinct world, engaged in nurturing activities, focused on children, husbands and family dependents".

During all of my life I have never considered the possibility of not ever having a child. What do I do with myself and what is my purpose on this earth if I am infertile? Can I have a role outside of that of a mother? Do I have the courage of Dr. Sarah and her sisters to go out into the world and make a place for myself outside of the protection of my husband?

My attitudes are colored by the fact that I did not experience the traditional family of mother, father and children living and growing together in my youth. Aunt Anna did a great job and I will be forever grateful to her, but I have always felt that I missed something. I would observe other families expressing love and happiness together. I dreamed of that for myself as a child and I still dream of that today. Dr. Sarah is correct in that there are other possible definitions for myself and my home in the world today but I think I will still make my best effort to exemplify "Home is a Cottage".

I think that Dr. Sarah is attempting to delicately indicate that a 'traditional' family may not be in my future. I must redefine my definition of family. I will increase my involvement in the community and in the store. I will help Fitch in any way that I can with his business. I will work harder to create a stronger 'family' of friends and neighbors in the community. Perhaps I am not putting enough efforts into my social life. Rather than going outside of my definition as housewife, I will try to expand life within my home. Perhaps it will be enough.

George

Volger's Jewelry is a thriving business in its new location. This spot is a hub of activity in the downtown due to its location next to the Interurban transportation station. It was great fun to watch all of my father's former customers come into the store to congratulate him on his retirement and to wish him luck. For years, many of them have conversed with Dad about their troubles on a weekly if not a daily basis. He served as their primary counselor. They continue to seek out his advice in my shop and usually purchase an item in gratitude. It most certainly will make a difference in holiday sales when his friends choose to spend their holiday funds in my store.

The greatest event to occur this year both in my life and that of my family was the birth of my son, George Volger III, on April 16th. (The Muscatine Journal, April 16, 1914, pg 9, "A New Boy Jeweler Arrives On Scene") This is the first child of Helen and myself and we hope that he will be the first of many. We have been so excited about the arrival of this little one. Helen and Mom have been sewing and knitting baby blankets and baby clothes and they have a room all prepared for baby Volger. Many of Helen's friends have had baby showers, and as a result, the baby bedroom is already stuffed with assorted items.

I celebrated his arrival at the store the evening of his birth with boxes of cigars that were open on the jewelry cases and available to all well wishers in the downtown area. A tremendous throng of them visited me at the store and continued the next day and for most of the week. What a wonderful celebration this was. I spend my days with a store full of happy and loyal customers whose purchases are plentiful and then I go home to my sweet little baby boy.

I spent the two months before the arrival of little George designing, building and donating the largest clock this community has ever seen, to the Ball Park. The face of the clock is more than six feet in diameter. It is being put directly in the back of second base within a few feet of the fence. An important feature is that the movement of the clock is detachable and will be installed before each game and removed immediately afterwards. It is thought that the clock will make the local ball park famous throughout the country.

The clock is being tried out at the local park and if the idea proves successful, similar clocks will be installed by the Elgin clock people, in all of the big league parks in the country. (The Muscatine Journal, April 13, 1914, pg 7, "LARGE CLOCK BEING INSTALLED AT PARK") The benefits of this gift are two-fold: I can pay my sports community back for the multitude of rewards that have come to me due to my participation in sports and it is a marketing strategy that has gotten my store wide notice in the media and throughout the community. Every time a sports fan looks at the time at the ball park, he or she will be reminded of my business.

I also view this clock as a tribute to the future of little George. Athletics has been an important part of my life and my father and mother have always provided all of the support and encouragement needed for a son to excel. I will help my son take advantage of all of the opportunities that life affords him and I expect that many of those will be in the practice of athletics. He already seems so smart and so coordinated and strong to me. I can only imagine how bright will be his future. Helen says I am crazy.

Through the happiness of these times, I have noticed a coldness emanating from Fitch Swan. I have seen him at various events in public and have noticed that he has been avoiding me. He always makes certain that he is at the opposite side of the room, when I am present. My thought was that I was imagining things until the birth of my son. I was shocked that he never came into my store to congratulate me. He never stopped by, called or sent me a card.

Perhaps he does not experience business competition in the same way that I do. He has taken to referring to me as the 'Boy Jeweler' and himself as the 'Experienced, Trusted Jeweler' in his advertising. (The Muscatine Journal, May 17, 1913, pg 5, Advertisement) He seems to define this as a personal battle. I do not have negative feelings toward him any more than I have had against ball players on opposing teams. He clearly feels no joy or excitement in rivalry.

This is troubling. He is the man that gave me a job when I needed one. He trained me in the field of jewelry making and watch repair. I feel gratitude toward him but he seems so aloof that I cannot figure out how to make him aware of this. Perhaps I can use Elsie to convey the message for me. Elsie, of course, came to the store personally to congratulate me on the birth of my son. She brought a plate of Aunt Anna's sweets and told me how she envied me and how much she wanted a child also. I feel some sympathy for Fitch's inability to father a child.

On the other hand, I do not know how I am expected to conduct my business under these circumstances. I have a son now and I can't afford to stop marketing my business. I cannot intentionally fail, nor can I send customers away. I cannot make my own business fail so that his can succeed. His attitude is beginning to make me angry. This makes no sense.

Chapter 5: 1915
Fitch

The tick-tock-tick-tock of the clocks echoed in my ears as I locked the daily proceeds in the safe, summoned my car and was driven home. When I walked through the spacious front porch of "Sheltering Oaks" I thought of how much I enjoyed having built a home that actually possessed a name of its own. That is a real sign of status.

Elsie loves this house and enjoys sharing it with others. Therefore I was not surprised to find a group of ladies gathered, chatting and giggling while they engaged in needlework. They were making every effort to keep their fingers clean enough to hold needles while eating dainty sandwiches and treats that Elsie had prepared. The home was full of bright pastel colors with sweet scents emanating from all available surfaces. She had decorated with spring flowers for the occasion and each guest was given yellow jonquils as they departed. It seems she is always in the process of planning some gathering or event.

The problem with this effort on Elsie's part was that it was occurring while I contemplated retirement. I want to get out from under it all. I am tired of working so hard for so little. I am tired of competing with a young man whose biggest attainment in life has been the bouncing and throwing of balls.

My plan is to sell my business and to make enough money through that sale to quietly settle all of my debts. Considering my age, this effort would just appear as normal behavior to the community. Cornelius could close his present store and buy my business at a great price, move into my space with my stock and, with some of my assistance, would manage the entire enterprise.

I will have an auction sale on May 26th and will advertise I am 'Retiring' from business and that Cornelius is taking over. I will advertise that the entire $50,000 stock is now on sale as well as all fixtures and furniture. I will promise that 20 free presents will be given to the first twenty ladies that attend. I announced in the newspaper, in bold print that I am '**Positively going out of Business**'. (The Muscatine Journal, May 26, 1915, pg 6, Swan Advertisement)

Cornelius would profit by the increased community interest. He could have a 'going out of business' sale in his old store while I am have a 'going out of business' sale in mine. He could then have a 'grand opening' sale in my store. This seems like a foolproof plan to me.

****

Unfortunately I did not make enough money in that sale to settle my debts and I therefore found that I could not afford to go out of business. Instead, I continued on with my effort to develop a strategy to sell more and to sell more profitably. The people of Muscatine did not seem to notice that I had stated that I was "positively going out of business". They were just glad to have my store remain open so that they could continue to stop by to look at all the lovely watches and gems and to drink a cup of coffee and chat with me. Occasionally they would purchase some small item in an effort to keep me in operation. I think that their purchases often do not pay for the coffee that they drink and the cookies that they consume. They just do not understand the underlying cost of sustaining a retail business.

Poor Cornelius had quite a few anger outbursts throughout all of this uncertainty and change. I invited him and my sister Harriet to a meeting in the back room of my store on a Sunday afternoon to discuss the situation. I was completely honest with them and informed them that my profits from the 'going out of business' sale were not sufficient to pay off the bills of the jewelry store and that I did not feel it proper to dump all of these unpaid bills on Cornelius. This made sense to them and they agreed that we would all work together to try and improve the store's profitability so that it would be worthwhile for Cornelius to take it over eventually. We agreed that we would not let the information of our economic difficulties get into the community. People might stop buying at Swan's Jewelry if they think they cannot get a fair price.

I did notice that the 'going out of business' and 'auction' strategies resulted in a higher level of sales. This would become a major part of my new marketing plan. The word 'sale' has a great impact on people. They do not seem to realize that prices can be raised one day so that they can be listed as 'sale' items the next. The concept of 'auction' has a similar impact. It is also not uncommon to bring in merchandise that is of a lower quality and price to sell at the auctions. This is a profitable business plan.

****

Towards the end of the summer I began gearing up for the upcoming holiday season. I had located some fine new gems to put on display in my window beginning in early November. Although I had plenty of stock on the shelves for the holiday sales, I had become quite sensitive to Volger's advertisements suggesting that my stock was dated. I thought that if I was very strategic with my holiday spending I could make some profits this year and ease some of the financial stress.

The new pieces arrived in early October and I was certain I had made the right selections. This jewelry was beautiful and the people of Muscatine will recognize that and snap it right up. I had saved much of the ornamentation from Elsie's prior Christmas decoration efforts. I was feeling so optimistic during the week that I had dug them out of my storage area and attempted to adorn the store with those decorations myself. I had even saved Elsie's Santa picture that had caused me to be the focus of so much ridicule last year. I pinned it to its prior location on the back curtain.

As I was driven home, I noticed the cool scent of autumn in the air. I had the car steered beneath the russet maples and golden elms that lined the street and looped along the river. I watched the flocks as they moved south along the flyway. Today the water stretched in long languid pools. A heron stood watch from a rock near the eastern bank. I would at times become mesmerized by the sights and sounds of the river. It spoke to the artist that existed within me.

When I arrived home, I glanced at the mirror in the vestibule as I took off my coat and hat. I look a lot more like Santa this Christmas than I did last. A carefree evening downtown is just what we need tonight. It will be my revival. Perhaps we need to do this every couple of weeks. If this stress continues, I will look like Santa's Grandfather before long.

As I walked into the dining room I saw Elsie pouring over a pile of papers again. "Another party, Elsie?" I asked.

"I am going to give one of the most beautiful Christmas parties that this neighborhood has ever seen."

"Oh, Elsie, I don't think that I have the energy for a house full of guests this holiday season."

"It's okay, Fitch. I am just inviting a group of lady friends so that it will be smaller than our usual holiday party."

****

While I attempted to work my way through the pathetic December business sales, Muscatine passed an ordinance on the16th, creating a professional fire department and calling for the volunteer hose companies to be disbanded. (* Bender, Alex, *Muscatine Fire Department* : 128 years of dedication, Muscatine, IA : s.l. 2003, pg 31) Just like that. Years and years of knowledge and experience of the local volunteers disbanded. Society today does not value the know-how that a lifetime of effort yields. I don't think they will find a paid professional that has the knowledge of hose operation that I have gained over time.

These courageous volunteers throw themselves into the heat and flames of life out of the desire to help their fellow man. They seek neither reward nor recognition for themselves. They wish to protect their neighbors and to care for their community. That type of dedication and commitment cannot be paid for.

I believe that this represents the increasing control of government over the business of its citizens. Government wants to regulate what occurs in every fire company. It has a need to dictate every action and to manage all expenditure. The present system has operated well for over 40 years without that level of central control. The bodies of government do not have the knowledge and the experience to know what needs to be purchased, nor what responses need to be taken in emergencies. The entire department will now be composed of a chief and 12 firemen. (Bender, Alex, *Muscatine Fire Department* : 128 years of dedication, Muscatine, IA : s.l. 2003, pg 32) I do not think that they can manage the fire emergencies with the efficiency that the individual companies have. I guess we will see.

I find myself sinking deeper and deeper into the mud. I walked to the river yesterday in hope of raising my spirits. I watched an old, faded turtle burying itself into the mire.

You and I are just alike, my friend, I thought. *Nobody has any use for us anymore. We are old and tired and instead of valuing our knowledge and honoring our contributions, this world of young people is kicking us in the behind. They want us to disappear into the sludge so that they can take ownership of all that we possess.*

Muscatine Hotel

Elsie

We have all been watching the construction of the new Hotel Muscatine with wonder and awe. It is a few blocks from Fitch's store, near the railway station and across the street from the Mississippi River. Every time I walk down the avenue, it is taller and more splendid. The building is of red brick with light cream color sandstone trim. I am not familiar with the architect but he sure knows what he is doing in that it blends into the beauty of the river. It is planned to open in April and Fitch and I have been invited to the inaugural banquet and ball on April 8th. (The Muscatine Journal, April 9, 1915, pg 4, "VISITORS OF PROMINENCE AT THE HOTEL INAUGURAL")

This is going to be a first-class event with only the finest people in the area invited as well as many business people from out of town and out of state. I hear that around 300 guests are expected. The banquet will include a nine course dinner and there will be various venues in which to dine with musical entertainment, followed by an evening of ballroom dancing. (The Muscatine Journal, April 9, 1915, pg 4, "VISITORS OF PROMINENCE AT THE HOTEL INAUGURAL")

I picked up some deep green embroidered silk fabric when I was last in Paris and have saved it for such an occasion. My dressmaker was thrilled to have such lovely material for her work. I gave a swatch to Wilson Shoe Store across the street from Fitch's and Mr. Wilson has had a pair of matching silk pumps made for me. Of course, I was able to select the best jewelry in town for the evening.

Fitch is also looking forward to the event and has been working with his tailor to have special evening attire designed. He has an impeccable sense of style and attention to detail. He keeps himself perfectly groomed and his store spotless. It is an important part of his image. He also believes that such fastidiousness keeps him looking vital and young. Perfection, neatness, precision. All of those traits are highly valued by Fitch.

In fact, as I marveled at the beauties of Europe during our recent trip he expressed disappointment by the dirt and filth that he observed. It blocked his perception of the wonder of the continent itself.

Thus I have always left the construction of his attire to him and his tailor because of the difficulty in meeting Fitch's exacting standards. However, this evening his tailor hit it right on the mark. He laughed when I told him that I thought he looked like a member of the royal family. He pulled me in front of the mirror with him and said that we could have been mistaken for the royals if we were in the right location. He mentioned that we probably need the wealth of the royalty to pay for our attire.

Our chauffer drove our Cadillac to the porch to pick us up and delivered us to the front step of the hotel where we were greeted by the hotel owners and developers. We were escorted into the magnificent lobby area that was filled with guests in sparkling evening attire. All of the areas of the hotel were open for touring, with an employee available to provide information on the many unusual features.

I was impressed by the fact that all of the 125 hotel rooms were outside rooms with windows. It is so important in the summer time especially, to be able to open windows and benefit by the flow of air. Nearly every room had a bath and toilet but all were equipped with hot and cold running water. There was a cafe and lunch room that would serve the community as well as the residents of the hotel. A beautiful sun parlor overlooked the Mississippi, along with a banquet and ball room. The basement held Turkish bath parlors, a 5 chair barber shop and a billiard room. (The Muscatine Journal, April 9, 1915, pg 32 Advertisement)

When we found our assigned dining location, I was delighted to find that we were seated at the same table as George Volger and his wife, Helen. It seems that we were organized according to business category. This gave me an opportunity to find all about what life is like with the new baby George. Helen and I chatted away. She talked about how much it helped her to have George's parents available to assist with the baby and assist with the business when needed. My goodness, these people seem to have everything that anybody could ever want.

We were told that it has recently been announced that George will take over management of the Muskies basketball team. This has created quite a stir in the community. Fitch sat silently while people gathered around to congratulate George and discuss his future plans for the team.

Finally, dinner was served and everybody moved to their seats. George mentioned the ice boxes that he had seen during the tour. "Did you notice that they have seven big ice boxes that keep things cold without any ice? (The Muscatine Journal, April 9, 1915, pg 19, "7 BIG ICE BOXES WITHOUT ANY ICE")

"Have you ever heard of such a thing?" asked George.

"I don't see how that will work," responded Fitch.

"Evidently there is some sort of oil or something that circulates through coils in the back. It is all run by electricity. One of the modern marvels of the world," George responded.

"I am not sure that they have thoroughly considered the problems with such a plan," said Fitch. "How are you going to know if adequate cold is being maintained? When you look in an ice box you can see the ice melting and that tells you about when you need to add more to retain the proper temperature. In addition, the fact that it runs on electricity is idiotic when you consider the lack of dependability of electricity. You are basically going to have constant problems with the system."

"I am thinking that you do not have much faith in modern technology, Mr. Swan."

"I am thinking that people will be eating a lot of spoiled food," said Fitch.

"Mr. Swan, in the basement they have a big motor ice cream freezer without ice.

No provision has been made for any ice compartment. The freezer too is connected with the refrigerating plant and the same circulating brine does the work." (The Muscatine Journal, April 9, 1915, pg 19, "7 BIG ICE BOXES WITHOUT ANY ICE")

"Your statement is false upon its face. Ice cream without 'ice' is not 'ice' cream, George. I don't know what you would call such a thing but it cannot be called 'ice' cream. That makes no sense at all. More time in the classroom and less time in the gymnasium might have given you more competence."

"Oh, I don't know, Mr. Swan, it seems to me that my level of competence is providing me with some success," replied George.

At that point, Helen interrupted and suggested that George finish with his meal so that they might be able to join the dancing. Fitch concentrated on his meal; George gulped down his food and swept Helen onto the dance floor where they remained for the rest of the evening.

On our way home, I couldn't help but to mention to Fitch how the Volgers seem to have everything. They have a child and they both have involved parents, and he has his sports career and his business. Fitch advised me that George is riding for a fall. His ongoing interest in playing games has inflated his business success and once everybody discovers the lack of precision and dependability of his work, his business will lose air. He said that you cannot develop the level of skill that he has in the few years of experience that George has. He is misrepresenting himself and the public will soon find that to be the case. It shows a lack of regard and respect for those who have spent a lifetime developing their skills to a high level.

****

Fitch planned his retirement from the jewelry store this year. (The Muscatine Journal, May 24, 1915, pg 4, "Pioneer Jeweler to Retire From Trade") He is sick of it all. He planned to sell it to Cornelius at a very low price to help establish him in a successful enterprise. He wanted to work with him to get things on a very good footing and then he would slowly withdraw his attentions and focus them more on enjoying leisure time. We planned to visit the spots that we have always dreamed about and he wanted to focus more attention on his boards and volunteer work. He especially wanted to spend more time with the Alert Hose Company because it provides him with such a sense of purpose.

This plan was never realized. After all of the advertising and planning and after Cornelius sold his business and moved into ours, Fitch found that he was unable to move forward. He did not make enough money at his closing out sales and auctions to pay the bills that are owed by the store.

I was rather embarrassed by the whole situation and my friends kept asking me what had happened. I, of course, did not want to inform them that Fitch was having financial problems at the store so I said that Fitch so loved working with Cornelius and Cornelius with him, that neither wants to part. They will continue to work together as long as possible.

Then Fitch started having auctions, some of them even called 'going out of business' auctions over and over and over. My friends stopped asking me about any of this business behavior. I felt that they were looking at me with pity in their eyes.

I tried to discuss this all with Fitch but he would cut off the conversation by saying that there were some things about business that I did not understand. He suggested that I focus my attention on my volunteer activities and home. My suggestions increased, rather than relieved, his anger.

Fitch was also very upset about George being named the manager of the Muskie basketball team. He felt it was an honor that he did not deserve and that he was only given the position because he donated that, what Fitch calls, 'the vulgar Volger' clock at the ball park.

It is all piling up for him. George in charge of the team, George with a son, crowds going into George's store to shop rather than his own.

****

The Alert Hose Company has been disbanded. This has struck Fitch like a knife through the heart. I know that he understands the need for a professional fire department at an intellectual level but he is having difficulty dealing with the emotions of it all. He has devoted much of his free time to the Alert Hose Company. Those volunteers are like family to him. Fitch has viewed his time as a fire fighter as vital to the safety and security of the neighborhood and the community. There seems to be nothing of enough significance to replace that endeavor.

If we could have a child, the world would be turned around for him. It strikes me that of his building list of grudges, it is the only one that I can do anything about. While touring the hotel, I paid particular attention to the

Turkish health baths. Perhaps that is what I need. I have made another appointment with Dr. Sarah to get her view of the advertised health benefits.

"How is life treating you, Elsie? Have you given any more thought to the ideas that we have discussed in the past?"

"Dr. Sarah, Fitch decided to retire this year, as I am sure you read about in the paper. After tons of planning for our future in retirement, he has found that he cannot afford to do so. He is like a balloon that is being deflated. I need to take some helpful action in this situation. I absolutely need to have a child. It is the only thing that I can do to mend Fitch's life. It is the answer. I have no power to affect any other kind of change."

"Elsie, perhaps you might benefit by thinking less about fixing Fitch's life and more about enhancing your own. Do you really think that we can 'fix' each others lives? Doesn't each one of us have the responsibility for our own lives?"

"I don't mean to be rude, Dr. Sarah, but I am not up to one of your philosophical discussions today. I toured the new Hotel Muscatine the other day and I noticed that they have health spas or Turkish Baths. Health baths of every description are being offered. There are shower baths, tub baths, Turkish baths, sitz baths, kidney baths, needle baths and the new electric baths. I have heard that they are superior to the health baths in Battle Creek. Could they make me healthier and would that make me more likely to get pregnant?"

"I am sorry to tell you that those types of treatments will do nothing about pregnancy. They are most likely to help those who have various physical aches and pains or those who need to relax. They would probably do Fitch a lot of good. Elsie, there is no such easy answer to this."

"You know I have tried prayer. I am an avid member of the Baptist Church and am one of those people who does not need to be coaxed to go to church, but one who needs to be coaxed to leave. I am hoping that God will answer my prayers."

"Man cannot know what is in his future plan, Elsie. I do not know what your God wants for your future."

I think that the only real hope left to me is that of prayer. Dr. Emma and Dr. Sarah seem to have philosophical statements to offer and I fail to see how that is going to really impact anything. I feel that they are attempting to alter the way I think rather than alter the way my reproductive organs act.

The only entity that can alter my way of thinking is my God. These ladies do not understand what it is like to be alone in childhood and rather isolated from parents.

My evening family conversations were not with my human family, they were with God and his son, Jesus. Aunt Anna simply did not have insight into my feelings of loneliness.

Each night I would lie in my bed and say a prayer about my day. I would ask God to help me make my way through the next day. I would carry on conversations with the young boy, Jesus and with his father, God. I would ask for advice and comfort that I thought was appropriate for each, considering age. Jesus could enter my thoughts and help me figure out how to deal with various situations in my school and among my friends. God could help me deal with teachers, Aunt Anna, my seldom seen mother and my almost never seen father. I felt that they were in the room with me and I would fall asleep each night in their presence. They were my family.

I still get comfort today from going to church. It seems respectful to visit in the house of God and Jesus rather than expecting them to always come to mine. Fitch works most Sundays and doesn't like to attend church with me. I really don't mind because it allows me to continue my private bond. I won't speak to the doctors about my relationship with God. I don't think they would understand it. I think that if you tell people that you speak to God they will think that you are deranged. I could try to make it clear that I am no Carrie Nation who gets direct orders from on high. It is not a separate voice that I hear. God enters my thinking and I believe he moves my thoughts in positive directions. What I will do is be my own counsel, pray longer and harder and try to be a better person.

One of the ways I honored God was to have a Christmas party in honor of his son. My lady friends gathered in my home, which was decorated with poinsettias and ferns, in the afternoon to make Christmas gifts and tell Christmas stories. At 6:00, the doors of the dining room were drawn displaying the dining table which had a miniature Christmas tree as a centerpiece that bore a lighted candle for each member of the group. After dinner, each guest was requested to snuff out her candle and select a present from the pile at the foot of the tree. Then as the Edison phonograph played "Uncle Fritz's Christmas Party" the packages were opened in the living room, where Santa was sitting in the open fireplace with 'Seasons Greetings' in his arms. We spent the early evening singing along with Christmas carols played on the Edison.

George

I was able to accept the position of manager of the Muskies semi-professional basketball team because of the great team that I have at my store. Managing a business is more than selecting the right products. The success of any business has more to do with the development and management of people. Employees need to emotionally buy into the company. They need to feel that my success is also their success. The best way to do that is to operate a business like a ball team. Find the right person for the right position and then provide the support and resources needed for him to perform his task. I expect and trust my employees to always do their best and they know that. Because of that I am able to leave the business to them while I travel and work with the ball team.

There is simply no marketing plan that could prove more successful than my management of the basketball team. It causes my name to be before the public regularly and brings customers into the store to give me their assessment of team assets and defects. Of course there might be negative consequences to my business if the team does badly. I don't see that there is any chance of that. In both my business team and my ball team, we have the right players, the right management and the right plan.

Unfortunately the community found out about my selection as manager just before the inaugural ball of the hotel. Business people were assigned seating according to their product or profession. It was not the world's best seating arrangement when I found that Helen and I were seated next to the Swans.

It is always delightful to spend time with Elsie but Fitch is becoming more negative as the days go by and I think that the news about the ball team did nothing to improve his mood.

I tried to have a civil conversation with the man but it did not prove to be possible. I am truly getting sick of it.

He is now advertising as the 'truth teller', implying, I believe, that I am a liar. This is reminiscent of his past advertising of himself as the 'reliable' jeweler and me as the 'kid' jeweler. I was able to make a lot of profit off of the 'kid' jeweler label. When my son was born, the newspaper even labeled him as the 'kid' of the 'kid jeweler'.

Mr. Perfect will probably never be able to be introspective. If he cannot succeed at his business he needs to start looking at possible fault within himself rather than blaming me. As long as he is unable to analyze his own business behaviors and find where improvement needs to be made to make him more competitive, he will not get ahead. His need to assign himself an A grade for everything does not allow him to perceive any of his own faults or weaknesses. It causes him to have a kind of blindness.

Helen Volger

He was not able to clearly see what was going on around him at the Muscatine Hotel Inaugural. When Helen and I danced after the dinner, I observed that one man after another asked Elsie to dance and she consented. I could not believe that Fitch just sat there at the table and watched while Elsie was twirled about the room by various young and not-so-young men. Elsie needs to think about how this looks to the public and Fitch needs to get up off of his behind and get moving. If that was my wife, we would have had a major discussion at the end of the evening. He is not able to see a problem that is developing right before his eyes. As I said, he is blind.

Chapter 6: 1916
Fitch

My business did not make enough money to support both Cornelius and myself. It took a while to accept this fact. He searched for a job but was not successful. By the Christmas season he was selling Edison phonographs in a store that he rented across from mine. (The Muscatine Journal, December 14, 1916, pg 7, Advertisement) His leaving my establishment saddened us both but I was grateful that he was only a few steps away from my location. We were able to visit each other with frequency when business was slow, which unfortunately seemed to be rather often.

Elsie has gotten into this religious mind set. She keeps suggesting that I need to go to church more often. She thinks that it is the answer to all of life's issues. I have long been a supporter of the Church and Mollie was also. Religion does not appear to mean the same thing to me that it does to Elsie. She thinks that if she asks God for things, she will get them. She prays for this and she prays for that. Why would she think that her needs and wants would be prioritized by God? Why would her prayers be granted rather than the person who is praying for the opposite? Does God like her better?

There is no point in discussing this with her. I have found that it is often useless to discuss reason with people overtaken by religious emotions. At times it makes me rather angry. Why would she think that God did not answer my prayers when I asked for Mollie to live? Why would God deny the fervent prayers of both Mollie and myself when we asked for our little baby to survive? Does she think that our prayers and hopes had less significance to God than hers?

Although neither Elsie nor I are in favor of the consumption and sale of alcohol, we don't approach it with the religious fervor of a Carrie Nation. I don't think any God that exists cares one whit if I have or sell a drink. There are a lot bigger problems in the world for him to direct his attention towards. How about the conflicts in Europe? How about the increasing negativity that is being expressed toward recent immigrants to this country?

I think that praying to God is the easy answer. It sure is easier than putting a lot of thought into finding a solution to a problem. If mankind is totally messed up and the world explodes into a world war, it has nothing to do with the behaviors of the people on earth. It is God's will. Perhaps God will deliver me from a world war. Perhaps God will deliver me from George Volger. I think not.

****

I read in the newspaper that the 1916 ice harvest started on the 15th of January. One of the largest natural ice companies, Rosenmund and Kuebler, in Muscatine started cutting ice today from the river, about a half mile north of the High Bridge. (The Muscatine Journal, January 15, 1916, pg 8, "ICE HARVEST STARTS IN MUSCATINE TODAY") Cornelius' father was actually one of these ice harvesters who owned his own company. It is anticipated that the other ice companies will start their harvest soon also. The company said that the ice is between 10 to 12 inches thick and by tomorrow will be three or four inches thicker if the present low temperatures continue. The river ice this season is clear as crystal and is said to be better for packing than at any time during the past few years. Ice of lower quality has been harvested from the Muscatine slough for the past three weeks, but it is used only for companies that need heavy refrigeration. (The Muscatine Journal, January 15, 1916, pg 8, "ICE HARVEST STARTS IN MUSCATINE TODAY")

It is clear that the natural ice companies of Muscatine would not agree with George Volger and the Muscatine Hotel that their time has passed. I cannot imagine all of us getting rid of our ice boxes which use an available natural resource in order to rely on the 'ice boxes without ice' that they favor. I also cannot imagine the loss that would occur to all of the local businesses that harvest in Muscatine. With the reliability of electricity in our city I imagine that many of those hotel 'iceless ice' boxes are filling up with ice from the Mississippi river right now, not to mention the 'iceless ice-cream'.

****

Finally something good happened. Early in the year, the city baseball league was forming and George Volger sponsored and of course, managed a team called the Reliable Jewels and I sponsored the Swan's Diamonds, which was coached by Lee Fuller. (The Muscatine Journal, August 14, 1915, pg 5, "Announce Revised List of Eligibles") It was a great deal of fun to attend the games throughout the season and watch my team compete.

It was a surprise to find that in August, the Jewels and the Diamonds were to battle in the first game for the city championship. The game was played at the south lot, overlooked by the infamous 'vulgar Volger' clock. I spoke to my team before the game and advised them of the importance of winning. I pointed to the mega-clock and asked them if there was any chance that anybody could strike it with a baseball. I would give $1.00 to each player that struck the clock.

Not only did my team wipe out the 'Reliable Jewels' but they also managed to have a ball bounce off of the face of the clock. Upon seeing it deflected off of the monstrosity my team laughed and cheered and slapped the back of the player. George seemed a bit surprised by the reactions. He mentioned to my manager that the behavior of the team did not seem very sportsmanlike. I responded by yelling out, "Give it a rest, George, no damage was done to the clock. The boys were just having fun."

****

It was no more than 15 days into the New Year when my fears regarding the professional fire department became reality. The Lilly Dry Goods Store (the store in which Elsie worked when I met her) was destroyed by fire with a loss of about $30,000. Three other stores were damaged: the Chocolate Shop, Ruthenberg Clothing Company and the Iowa Panitorium. The estimated total loss was placed between $175,000 and $200,000. (Oelwein Daily Register, January 15, 1916, pg 1, "MUSCATINE HAS FIRE SATURDAY")

William Underdonk and his family, who were sleeping in an apartment above the store, were awakened by a large explosion that was accompanied with a wave of fire at 4:40 in the morning. The explosion, which occurred in the basement of the store cracked the windows on the south side of William's apartment and terrified his entire family. He immediately turned in the alarm. (The Muscatine Journal, January 15, 1916, pg 5, "Fire Destroys Store")

William said, "It seemed but a minute after I turned in the alarm that I heard the truck beneath my window. When I reached the street the firemen had one stream of water playing on the front part of the building. I at once, called their attention to the outbreak of flames in the rear where I believed the fire started and two streams of water were turned into the flames which belched forth from the office section of the establishment." Mr. Underdonk claimed that the entire rear part of the building was in flames. (The Muscatine Journal, January 15, 1916, pg 5, "Fire Destroys Store")

The city's two newly purchased Mack fire trucks were brought to the scene. They had been stored in a garage of the Muscatine Motor Car Company until members of the fire committee could properly test them later in the month. (Bender, Alex, Muscatine Fire Department : 128 years of dedication, Muscatine, IA : s.l. 2003, pg 31) They were not equipped fully and the trucks were sent to the outlying stations to secure a large amount of fire fighting paraphernalia. When it was discovered that the paid department's supply of firefighting equipment was not sufficient, trucks were dispatched from the old volunteer station with additional hose. In response to a second alarm, many volunteer fire fighters gathered and assisted in fighting the blaze. (The Muscatine Journal, January 15, 1916, pg 5, "Fire Destroys Store")

At 7 o'clock two of the fire trucks were dispatched to obtain additional apparatus and emergency hose to South Muscatine. The truck ran out of gasoline and the tank had to be refilled before it was able to return to the fire.

The city's fire committee evaluated the new trucks after the Lilly fire. They were taken to several slippery and hilly streets to test their ability to climb. The alderman who was the chair of the fire committee deemed the vehicles satisfactory but as he was about to give his statement to the council, it voted to accept and discuss the recommendations behind closed doors. When they emerged, they had decided to reject the new vehicles.

It is assumed that Chief Brown, upon observing the capabilities of the trucks at the scene of the fire, found them to be not satisfactory. (Bender, Alex, Muscatine Fire Department : 128 years of dedication, Muscatine, IA : s.l. 2003, pg 31)

After the council had adjourned, some members of the fire committee admitted that it was felt that the trucks did not have sufficiently powered engines. The members of the committee thought that the trucks' bodies were too heavy and particularly so, when loaded with equipment.

This is exactly what I predicted. The purchase of inadequate equipment by a governmental group that did not know what it was doing. Hoses and equipment stored away from the trucks which were not parked in a central location. Not enough fire fighters, not enough gasoline put in a truck. It's a wonder the whole community did not burn down.

Then, the city council needs to discuss this in a closed session? They did not want the public to hear of their incompetence and over reaching. This is proof of the inefficiency of centralized authority and power. There is no going back to the volunteer system of course. Although it was proven to be successful over 40 years, once government has taken control, it will never relinquish that control.

Elsie

I was so saddened by the news of the Lilly fire. I spent many hours working inside of that beautiful building. Countless memories of great times and wonderful co-workers existed within its walls. It is the last place that I was employed before I married Fitch.

I read in the paper that it is believed that gas developed and was trapped in the basement by banking the coals in the furnace to retain heat. The gas exploded and ignited a huge fire that overcame the building. Thank heaven that the fire department was able to stop the flames with the loss of only that building rather than an entire block. It is impressive how a brand new fire department with brand new equipment was able to contain the fire before it ate up more of the Muscatine business district.

The day after the fire, I took the streetcar downtown to see what was left of my old store. As I got off at the station, I noted that a rather large crowd had gathered to view the remains, even though it was a cold and dreary January day. As I walked near, a group of men and women called out to me. They were my past fellow workers.

We gathered close together to ward off the cold, and talked about all of our memories. Many of them still worked at the store and were frightened about the need to find another retail job in January. They were quite aware that January is a difficult month in which to find work. We shed a few tears and comforted and hugged each other. It was so wonderful to see all of those people again and it is gratifying to see that they still consider me to be a part of their group.

I was surprised to see my old friend and supervisor David walk around the corner. He had wavy brown hair and the biggest brown eyes that I have ever seen on a man. He smiled as his workers gathered around him with questions about the condition of their employment. In his usual soft manner, he informed them that prospects did not look good, but he was sure Mr. Lilly would want to

119

speak with them soon, when he had finished assessing the situation. He encouraged everybody to stay calm and wait for notice from Mr. Lilly.

David then noticed me at the edge of the group. "Hello, Elsie," he said. "I have not seen you in a long time. I am sorry that we first meet again at such a sad occasion."

"David, how nice to see you again. I have missed our conversations. The supervisory meetings that I had with you included the best counseling I have ever had."

"We will all be going for a cup of coffee in about half an hour, Elsie. Why don't you join us?"

As we arrived at the restaurant, David slipped into the seat next to my own.

"How has life been treating you, Elsie?" he asked. "I have not seen much of you since your wedding to Mr. Swan."

"All is okay, David."

"Just okay? With your big house and all of your jewelry and the Cadillac and all, life is simply okay?" he said.

"Money isn't everything, David. Family is more important to me and, in case you have not noticed, I don't appear to have any children."

"Are you wanting to have children?"

"It probably is not proper to discuss this with you, David, but I think that the love of children and the love of family is the only thing that can make me happy."

"I am sorry to hear that it is not working out for you. I have never thought about having children myself. My life has been full with my responsibilities at the store and the dog business that I operate. Although the dogs are a lot of labor, it is hard to feel lonely when you have those welcoming happy yips and the little tails wagging when you arrive home. I can't imagine how I could find the time or the energy for an actual child.

Have you ever tried a puppy, Elsie?"

"You can't be serious," I replied. "Who in their right mind thinks that a puppy is a substitute for a child?"

"But, really, have you ever tried having a pet, Elsie? Sometimes it is good practice for having a child. A pet needs attention, affection and care. It can also provide a lot of love. It could prepare you for the rewards and responsibilities of motherhood or could give you a taste of the trials and tribulations of parenthood. My dog actually had puppies and I would be glad to give you one."

"Dear God, you are serious, aren't you?"

"Yes I am. I will deliver her to your house tomorrow if you are interested."

"What kind of a dog is it, David?"

"It's a fluffy little white thing. I don't know what you would call it. It's a mutt of some kind but really kind of cute."

"I can't believe I am saying this, David, but bring it over tomorrow. What can it hurt? If I don't like having her, you will take her back, right?"

"Sure," said David, "and it will give me a chance to see that big mansion of yours."

The next afternoon, David brought over a beautiful little fluffy puppy with white curly fur and short ears. The moment it saw Aunt Anna, it ran over and sat in front of her, reached out a paw and whimpered to be picked up. Aunt Anna scooped the dog up and petted it while it nestled contentedly in her lap.

"I cannot believe this house, Elsie," said David. "This has got to be the most beautiful home in this town."

"I don't mean to be immodest but I do think that it is," I replied.

"Fitch had this designed to suit my needs and tastes. It looks like the puppy will be happy to stay with Aunt Anna while I give you a tour."

As we toured the house he said, "You know, Elsie, the puppy is going to need to have a place to sleep and some food to eat. You will need to think of a name for her and take her outdoors to relieve herself. I wouldn't just open the door and let her loose because she will probably run towards the nearest squirrel and you will never see her again."

When we returned to the parlor Aunt Anna had placed plates of cookies on the end table along with cups of steaming hot chocolate. David made himself comfortable before the fire and we spent the afternoon catching up on the occurrences of our lives since I left Lilly Store and married Fitch.

Aunt Anna joined us and advised me that dinner would soon be ready and that Fitch would soon be returning from the store. She asked David, "What does the little thing like to eat?"

"Primarily meats," he replied. "Even though they are incredibly delicious, I do not think I would feed her those cookies. It is not a good idea to feed a dog a lot of food that contains sugar.

"Elsie, the puppy has recently been removed from her mother and I would like to bring her mother over to visit a couple of times a week. Perhaps we could take her and her mother for walks."

"Oh my goodness," I said, "I surely would not want to keep her away from her mother. That would be too mean."

"What do you think you will name her?" he asked.

Aunt Anna responded, "I have the perfect name for her. She looks just as white and fluffy as sugar. I think we should name her Sugar."

David said, "I think it may have been pre-ordained, Anna, her mother's name is Cookie."

"Sugar it is then," I replied.

Sugar

Just as David was about to leave, Fitch arrived home. He walked into the foyer, took off his coat, hat and scarf and hung them on the rack. "Fitch, do you remember my former supervisor at Lilly's, David Porter?"

"Hi, David. Yes I do remember you." At that point Sugar came running into the room. "But I do not remember you," said Fitch.

"David has been kind enough to give me Sugar the puppy for a trial run. He owns her mother, Cookie and we will be taking the dogs for walks together for awhile. It is a good idea to keep that mother/child bond going as long as possible."

"Oh my!" exclaimed Fitch. "We are already referring to the puppy as a child, are we? I can hardly stand to think of what you will be calling her a month from now."

"That is, if I decide to keep her, Fitch," I responded.

"Oh, Elsie, you will decide to keep her."

George

Managing the Muskies has taken more of my time than anticipated but it is a great job. My employees' proficiency allows me to focus on interests outside of the business. When I observe how other businessmen manage their employees I often wonder if they have ever considered the amount of freedom that they would gain if they were able to provide a sense of empowerment to them. It seems that many feel that they would lose something by sharing some control with their staff. In reality it works in the opposite way. An employee who feels a sense of importance in the company and identification with the company has great value to the team.

The dynamics are similar with the ball team. I am fortunate to have competent staff and some of the most dedicated players that I have ever seen. They are bright, well disciplined and highly motivated. It just doesn't get any better than that. We are poised for a winning season.

****

The Lilly building was the victim of some type of explosion in its heating system. It is common for winters to include virtually continuous fires throughout the community, but they generally are not explosive in nature. The Lilly explosion blew flames and coals and cinders into neighboring buildings and was a threat to my store and the downtown business district. (The Muscatine Journal, January 15, 1916, pg 1, "Fire Destroys Store") We were very fortunate to have the professional fire department up and running. Even though they had little chance to practice with the new equipment before the fire, they were able to contain the blaze within the day. There were some operational problems which, I am certain, will be overcome within a short period of time but there is simply no question that professional management of such an important community function is a tremendous asset. There needs to be central command

and control of such a massive and important community resource. The prior volunteer fire groups were operated too much like neighborhood social clubs. If my home is on fire, please send me a trained, skilled and professional fire department.

****

Speaking of fires, rumors have been spreading that Elsie Swan has been observed having coffee downtown with David Porter and one person reports that he has even seen David walk into Elsie's home. David is in management at Lilly's and is also known to run a kennel. I am certain that it is one of those places that breeds half starving animals who are stuffed into tiny cages. He may be fortunate that he has been branching into the 'capitalizing on the misery of animals' business, now that the Lilly store has blown up. He is sure to need another job.

I think that I will not speak to Cornelius about this because he seems to take no action in response to my concerns. He has to spend a lot of time with both Mr. Swan and Elsie and I can only imagine how difficult that is for him with the continually modifying business relationship between himself and his uncle. This is most certainly one of the reasons for his temper outbursts. If I add more pressure about what is probably going on 'behind the scenes' of his beloved uncle's marriage, he will have more discomfort. I do not want to make life more difficult for him. I consider him to be one of my best friends.

Chapter 7: 1917
Fitch

I have begun to emphasize the sale of ladies' handbags and purses at the store. Actually Elsie suggested this as a possible way to increase foot traffic. She informed me that ladies often purchase handbags to match each of their outfits and that more money is spent on handbags than I ever thought was the case. I am hopeful that this will improve business. I need something positive to happen in that location.

I had an unpleasant experience in the business towards the end of September. Two young men entered my establishment during my busiest hours on Saturday evening, and one of them asked to see some watches. He indicated that he wanted to purchase one. I lifted a tray containing about twenty gold watches from the jewelry case and placed it on the counter. I then turned my back to the couple in order to obtain the knife that I used to open the backs of the watches to allow customers to look at the working mechanisms. Upon turning back around I noticed that one of the watches was missing. At the same time, it appeared that the customer's companion had left the store. I called the night officer and he immediately searched the present party, but did not find the stolen watch. (The Muscatine Journal, September 20, 1917, pg 10, "WATCH STOLEN SATURDAY NIGHT")

Upon reading the newspaper a couple of days later I noticed that the customer had talked to a reporter about the incident. He denied that he was accompanied to my establishment by anyone. He said, "I resent very much the effort made to connect me with the activities of a thief." The man was evidently employed by the railroads as a locomotive fireman.

(The Muscatine Journal, September 20, 1917, pg 10, "WATCH STOLEN SATURDAY NIGHT") Now this does not make me look good. I find it hard to understand how the paper could feel justified in publishing the comments of this man which do nothing but defame my character, when he was the man who came into my store with a thief. What is this world coming to?

At about the same time I observed a man defacing the sod on Weed Park. I, as the Park Commissioner, am aware of the cost and the effort that is required to maintain the grounds of the park in its excellent condition. Since it is next to my home and provides scenic views of the Mississippi, I often walk through it.

During one such stroll, I noticed a man who appeared to be removing sod from the Indian mounds area. I, of course, made a citizen's arrest. Charles Burroughs of Locust Street appeared in police court on charges of taking sod from the park due to the charges that I had filed. Burroughs was released upon payment of the costs and agreement to re-sod the area that he had de-sodded. (The Muscatine Journal, July 10, 1917, pg 4, "In Police Court") Thus once again, my name is in the police report section of the newspaper.

Taken in its totality, things are becoming very unpleasant in this world. There seems to be some kind of evil cloud sinking down upon us all. Something wrong is happening with people. It is not just in this town and in my business but it appears to be happening all over the world.

We are seeing this also in Europe which is the focus of much conflict and turmoil. It appears that we may be sucked into the vortex of that evil tornado. I have always believed that the United States needs to stay out of the affairs and problems of other countries and focus on the meeting of our own needs. There is a major advantage to being separated by an ocean from Europe and in occupying a separate continent which we lose if we dive into any problem that Europe experiences. There is no question that there is trouble overseas but when has there ever not been trouble overseas? The present unrest is a European problem and this is therefore a European war.

The United States has been making the utmost effort to remain out of this war for quite a long time. In fact as early as May 7, 1915 Germany sank the British liner the Lusitania which resulted in the death of 128 of our fellow Americans. (http://history1900s.about.com/cs/worldwari/p/lusitania.htm, "Sinking of the Lusitania")

I was pleased when President Wilson hesitated to involve us in the debacle and said that "America is too proud to fight" but demanded that Germany cease attacking ocean liners. Wilson also warned Germany that the US would not tolerate unrestricted u-boat attacks on the open seas. Although Germany agreed to stop such attacks, in January 1917 they were resumed with the knowledge that it would draw the US into the conflict but hoping that Britain would be defeated long before the US could mobilize.

My reluctance to US participation in the war crumbled with the disclosure of a telegram from German Foreign Minister Zimmermann to a German diplomat in Mexico. (The Muscatine Journal, March 1, 1917, pg 1, "CONGRESS IS STIRRED TO ACTION BY GERMAN PLOT") This was a message to the governments of Mexico and Japan, inviting them to be their allies in a war against the United States. Germany promised to finance the Mexican war effort and to return Arizona, New Mexico and Texas to Mexico. The disclosure of this telegram stifled almost all opposition to the entry of the US into the war.

I was initially very skeptical of the veracity of this plot. I have been a follower and a supporter of Senator LaFollete from Wisconsin who has publicly and loudly expressed doubts about the information. It takes a rather major leap of common sense to believe that Germany is seeking to conspire with Mexico and Japan. This reads like a piece of fiction to me.

There was, however, no doubt left in my mind about our need to become involved in this war after I read the front page of the newspaper on Thursday, March 3rd. It confirmed that Congress was stirred to action by the confirmation of the alleged German plot. It indicated that the plot was revealed in a set of instructions from the German foreign minister Zimmerman to German Minister Von Eckhardt in Mexico City, which was transmitted through Count Von Bernstorff, late German ambassador here. The message indicated that Germany was confident that unrestricted submarine warfare was the instrument by which she would bring England to her knees.

This document dated, Berlin, January 19, 1917, the contents of which have for some time been in the possession of the United States government, shows plainly that Germany was conspiring with Japan and Mexico.

The message was sent by Zimmerman. It stated that:

"On the first of February we intend to begin submarine warfare unrestricted. In spite of this, it is our intention to endeavor to keep neutral the United States of America. If this attempt is not successful we propose an alliance on the following basis with Mexico: That we shall give general financial support and it is understood that Mexico is to reconquer the lost territory in New Mexico, Texas, and Arizona. The details are left to you for settlement. You are instructed to inform the president of Mexico of the above in the greatest confidence as soon as it is certain that there will be an outbreak of war with the United States and suggest that the president of Mexico, on his own initiative, should communicate with Japan suggesting adherence at once to this plan, at the same time, offer to mediate between Germany and Japan. Please call to the attention of the president of Mexico that the employment of ruthless

submarine warfare now promises to compel England to make peace in a few months." (The Muscatine Journal, March 3, 1917, pg 1, "BERLIN ADMITS WAR PLOT")

The disclosure of this document also helped stifle interest in Mexico in an enterprise of this nature. Having just gone through a border conflict with the US, the Mexican government did not think they could win such a conflict. In addition, there was a great deal of distrust in Mexico of the Germans' ability to deliver on their promises.

The document disclosure also caused Japan to swiftly deny any interest in the intrigue and to express support for the entry of the US in the war.

When Germany made the decision to torpedo all freighters going to Britain and its allies, they knew that sinking US ships and the subsequent loss of life would draw the US into the conflict but they thought they could starve Britain into submission before that could occur. This was a massive miscalculation as the US very quickly ramped up for war

It was after 7 US freighters were torpedoed and sunk by the German navy in addition to the disclosure of the message of Germany to Mexico and Japan that President Wilson called for war and Congress declared war on April 6, 1917. (https://en.wikipedia.org/wiki/First_World_War, "World War I")

A national draft was swiftly passed and soon the US was sending both troops and ships into the conflict at a far faster pace than Germany had anticipated. It was interesting that the US did not enter the conflict as a member of the so called Triple Entente, Britain, France, Russia and their partners, but as an "Associative Power" operating in cooperation with that group but not as a part of it. (https://en.wikipedia.org/wiki/First_World_War, "World War I")

****

I have been named as one of the directors of the home defense association and am therefore concerned about and involved in the security of the home front. I have been actively involved in the selling of war bonds and see this as part of my responsibilities in the home guard. We have scheduled regular meetings for the necessary planning of safety measures because it is clear to all of us that the threat to Britain is actually a threat to our world in that it is a threat to our values and our way of living.

It is with a heavy heart that I watch our young men say goodbye to their families and homes and head out to fight this war against humanity. They will not return, if they return at all, as the same Iowans. Their innocence, their hope will be gone.

I understand the toll that life can take upon a personality. I no longer possess the optimism of youth. I see now that humans are not the kind people of good intent that I presumed as a child. I always thought that if you treated people with kindness, you would receive kindness in return. It is so clear that the world does not operate in that fashion.

On the local level, look at the example of George Volger to whom I have never been anything but kind and supportive and observe how he is treating me in return. There is obviously a world full of Georges. Just think of it. We are in a world war. As hard as it is to believe, the entire world is actually at war. What does this tell us about humankind?

Elsie

The entire community is gearing up for war. Aunt Anna, in particular, has spent many a sleepless night worrying about the people of Germany. She keeps asking everybody she meets if they know anything new about what is happening in Europe. I read the newspaper with her every day that I am able, because I think it is easier for her to face the headlines when I am with her.

Of course, she was terribly upset when the March 3rd paper arrived. After reading the coverage, it was without doubt that we were going to enter the fight. We sat together quietly all afternoon and waited for Fitch to arrive home to discuss the headlines with us.

"You know, Aunt Anna, that I have never felt that we should involve ourselves with the conflicts of other countries and especially on continents that exist on the other side of the ocean," said Fitch. "You and I have often agreed about the necessity of our country to focus on the needs of its own citizens and to not waste its energies and resources on the issues of others. However, it is now clear that this European situation is different. It appears that Germany does not want to only defeat England, but that it also has its sights on our own country. It is conspiring against us, Aunt Anna and it poses a direct threat to our safety and to our way of life.

"I am certain now that we need to engage in this war. I intend to do everything that I can to help protect you and Elsie, our community and our country. You can feel safe and secure in that."

"Thank you, Fitch. If you think that it is the right thing for our country to do, I am sure that it is correct. I trust your judgment. Is there anything that I can do to help you in this effort?"

"The young men will soon be leaving the area. You and Elsie will have much planning to do with your women's groups. I am certain that the troops will need items that you can supply. Although it is hard to see at this time, it is likely that they can use knitted caps and quilted blankets and perhaps homemade cookies and candies and, I am very sorry to say, perhaps bandages."

"Fitch," I asked, "what do you see as the impact of all of this on the community? What do you think that we can expect?"

"Well, Elsie," he replied, "we will have a community of lonely young women and worried mothers and fathers as their young men go off to war. We can expect to see everybody listening for the news and searching for every new detail. I think that the churches will burst at their seams as more and more people pray for the safety of their loved ones. An interesting effect will also be that many of the jobs that these young men have will go empty. There will not be enough men left in the community to perform all of the work that there is to be completed. I am not certain what the result of that will be. Perhaps they will ask that you ladies perform their jobs while they are gone."

"Can you see yourself working in the button factory, Aunt Anna?" I asked. "I think I would like to work for one of the ice companies. I can imagine what it must feel like to slide around the icy river on boots, with the eagles flying overhead. I think I would love it."

"I don't think you have the muscles for that, Elsie," Aunt Anna replied. "I can't see how you could possibly pick up the heavy blocks of ice, even if I was there and tried to help you. I think that we would have to find a man's job that doesn't take a lot of muscle strength. We need to think of that. Surely there is some job that we could do?"

"It seems fortuitous that this comes at a time when I have been thinking of finding a meaning for myself that exists outside of the realm of the housewife."

"What are you talking about, Elsie? Are you not happy with our lovely home and the life that we have?"

"It's not that, Fitch. Many women are now finding careers and interests outside of the home. Perhaps this is an opportunity for me to do some searching."

"The things that you do around here are important to all of us, and the work that you do in your women's groups is important to the community. Don't sell yourself short, Elsie. I will see to it that you will never have to work outside of our home and that you will never experience financial need again. I will always take care of you and of you also, Aunt Anna. Do not fear. This war will make no difference in that regard."

****

Fitch was correct that the war effort created a lot of needs that could be met

131

by women working at home. We met as groups and made bandages and blankets. The newspaper had knitting patterns and lists of volunteers to teach or consult regarding problems. Of course, Aunt Anna became a cookie making machine and continually boxed up dozens to send to the troops.

David had found a new retail job and would stop by during his irregular off hours for our walks with Cookie and Sugar. Although it occasionally became rather tedious to accompany the dogs, I did not have the heart to say no especially when I observed how joyous they became upon seeing each other. They would jump and bark and yelp and snuggle.

I came to look forward to my walks with David and the dogs. It always included a lot of teasing and laughter. If we were not laughing at the dogs, we were laughing at each other. It was easy to communicate with David because he always listened to me carefully and responded with thoughtfulness and care.

It did occur to me that it was unusual for a married woman to walk around town with a young man. I mentioned to David that I had some concerns. He said such thinking was old fashioned and we could not let the suspiciousness of others cause Cookie and Sugar to be denied their time together.

David would often visit with Fitch upon our return, if he was at home. They seemed to enjoy each other's company. Fitch is taking so little pleasure in his relationships with his male friends that it was good to see him experiencing some enjoyment. I think that David is doing this for my benefit. He is aware that Fitch is suffering from a bit of malaise. I appreciate him but I think I may be beginning to appreciate his presence too much.

I find our conversations repeating in my mind as I lie in bed next to Fitch. My relationship with David is mixed with the joy, playfulness and light-heartedness of the bond between Sugar and Cookie. To think of them, to think of him, feels like a walk along the beach on a breezy day. I can feel the balminess of the sun and smell the sweet scent of wildflowers. More and more I am leaving this stormy, thundering, oppressive environment that I share with Fitch and returning to the warmth of my bond with David, Sugar and Cookie, that has come to exist within my soul.

I know that this is wrong but this private and secret life that exists in my head allows me to endure the trials of living with Fitch. I observe him sinking deeper and deeper into melancholy. The little joy and happiness that he experiences in his own life at this time does not provide him any extra to share with me. What does it hurt if my relationship with these living beings allows me to remain a supportive and understanding wife to Fitch?

George

My ball team members are reporting to me that they plan to join the war effort as soon as it becomes possible. I manage teams and arrange for games of teams in both basketball and baseball, most of which involve Iowa/Illinois teams. I spent several weeks in the early spring with the Chicago White Sox and the possibility of future professional connections for my players was paramount. However, all of these healthy young men are convinced that their homes are threatened by Germany, as well as possibly other countries. They are busy increasing their exercise and improving their eating habits so that they will pass the necessary military physical. Of course they will all pass with flying colors but it is touching to see them so concerned about being able to fulfill their responsibility to the war effort.

Congress declared war on April 6, and a national draft was swiftly passed and soon the US was sending both troops and ships into the conflict. The ball team was disbanded, as my young athletes were sent into war. Our last meeting was not without a few tears as they discussed how they must move beyond childish endeavors and apply the team building skills that they have learned in the sports world to the protection of the freedoms of this country.

Let me be the first to admit that we first and second generation German Americans are somewhat skeptical about this conflict. My family has had heated conversations around the dinner table and in the community about the 'real' meaning and reason for the war.

The majority in the US were hesitant to enter the war. I am a Democrat who supports President Wilson in many of his policies. In fact Wilson was re-elected (narrowly) in 1916 because he "had kept us out of the war". He was initially reluctant to bring the US into the conflict and my family shared in his reluctance. The revelation that Germany was attempting to ally with Mexico and Japan in early March was met with disbelief. This sounded like just the type of thing that a political movement would say to try and switch public sentiment. What could possibly arouse the resentments and fears of America more than a potential threat from Mexico? Clearly this was a set-up and would not stand the test of time.

With the subsequent documented admission of Germany to the plot, there was no question that remained in our minds. This has now been clearly demonstrated to be anything other than a trumped up anti-German plot. It looks like Germany wants to establish dominion over all of the earth, including us. Although we German people value the culture and the capabilities of the German heritage, we cannot let that happen. We value our freedoms.

****

In the midst of all of this sadness, Helen and I found a home for sale on Iowa Avenue that we purchased for our family. It is a sensible two story brick home in a friendly and well maintained neighborhood. It has enough space for us and possible future children and is well within our financial means. It is not gaudy and ostentatious but fits well within the character of the neighborhood.

What I love the most is the porch which stretches along the entire front of the home. Many of the houses bordering the street also have porches. In the Iowa summers it is common to spend much of your evening and weekend time on porches while neighbors walk up and down the avenue to visit each other. Not only do we experience some relief from the build-up of the day's heat in our homes, but we also stop and have an iced drink and catch up on the local happenings.

The good news is that in small town Iowa we always know what our neighbors are doing. The bad news is that in small town Iowa we always know what our neighbors are doing. It is good that our neighbors know when we are in trouble and when we need help. They will call us and inform us that Junior is walking across their back yard when he is supposed to be in school. They will inform us when the flour is cheaper in one store than another.

Because we have open windows most of the year and because our homes are close together, we often also know things we really don't want to know. We hear the disagreements that it does not benefit anybody for us to hear. We will know if Susie cannot behave herself in the classroom or if Mr. Smith is not arriving home until late in the evening. We have the shared knowledge that Sally never cleans her home thoroughly and that her family complains about the quality of dinner on a nightly basis.

During the porch visitation ritual, we not only find out about our own neighbors but also about most of the citizens in the community. Nearly everybody is related to everybody in small town Iowa. Upon meeting a new entrant into the community, one would ask of matters of heritage. "Are you related to Jimmy, who is the uncle of Sal, who is the cousin of George and the brother of Michael?" is a common conversational format. Through this method every individual is oriented in space and time. Through this method, however, rumors in small town Iowa can run wild.

Helen and I were relaxing on the porch one evening in August enjoying the dance of the lightning bugs. It was a hot evening and we were fanning ourselves and swiping at the attacking mosquitoes. Everybody had their own idea of how to keep the mosquitoes at bay. Helen is a fan of vanilla. She believes that the odor of vanilla is abhorrent to insects so she sprinkles herself, me and little George with it before we go outdoors. Although I am not certain that it actually works as intended, it does make us all smell tasty. Its effects were beginning to wear off and she was about to return to the kitchen for a second dose, when Connie from up the street stopped by with a plate of brownies.

"Have you heard anything about Elsie and David Potter lately?" asked Connie.

"No, I really haven't," replied Helen. "To what are you referring?"

"She has been seen around town with this man. They have been spotted eating lunch together and walking dogs. She does not seem to be aware that married women do not walk around town with men other than their husbands. I realize that she has not had the best upbringing in the world, and perhaps somebody better inform her that this is not proper behavior for a lady," said Connie.

"Oh my, Connie," replied Helen. "I sure would not be comfortable with such a conversation. It is all I can do to figure out how I am supposed to act. I don't think I am a person who should be educating others about proper lady behavior."

Connie said, "You sell yourself short, Helen. You are one of the finest ladies in this town."

****

When Helen and I were settling into our bed for the evening, I asked her if she really thought that Elsie is engaging in proper behavior for a lady of her station. "George, I was being honest when I told Connie that I am not in a good position to educate anybody about proper female behavior. Things are changing so much for women right now. More and more often they are needing to work outside of the home. We are hearing about movements that are advocating for the right of women to vote in the national elections. Add to that the fact that we have 3 of the first female medical doctors that were born in this community, I can tell you that change is the only certainty that I know."

"Not everybody is as open-minded and as clear thinking as you are, Helen. It is one of the reasons that I married you. I am concerned about what others are thinking and saying about Elsie. Perhaps someone needs to hint about these behaviors to Fitch Swan. He may be concerned about the impact on his own reputation and ultimately on his own business."

"George, I know that you mean well, but I think that you should stay out of this."

"But do you think she could be having an affair with this young man, Helen? Don't we have a responsibility to apprise Mr. Swan of that?"

"No we don't, George. I doubt very much that Elsie is having an affair and if she is, it is really not our business. Who knows what happens in the life of others? Who can judge what is proper or not proper behavior for them?"

Chapter 8: 1918
Fitch

A dark cloud of evil has descended upon this community. I can feel its heaviness, its essence in the air. I can hear its sigh. I am spending more of my free time sitting on the Indian mounds and contemplating the river. The Mississippi appears so smooth, even, and dependable from on high. It is when you are at its shore, close to its surface, that you can detect the conflict and turmoil beneath the slick shell.

It is the same with this community. We espouse patriotism, freedom, liberty and individual rights. We stand firmly upon each word and strictly interpret each phrase of our constitution. But as with the country as a whole, all is not so smooth beneath the surface.

Even in the best of times, it is difficult to absorb all of these immigrants that we have in our country. A common practice has been for those who came first to be suspicious of those who come later. Add a major world war with Germany into the mix of a local population that includes a large percentage of German immigrants and the river will begin to boil.

I am of German origin but my family has been here for several generations. My father was a contractor and a house builder. English was spoken in my home. Our religion was Methodist which included a congregation of mixed background. I am therefore considered to be 'American' in final evaluation.

Elsie is of mixed background, but Aunt Anna identifies closely with Germany and the German culture. She is quite concerned about what she perceives as increasing distrust and suspicion about people of German origin in the country as a whole, in this state and in this community.

When people in the community express their concerns about the Germans to me they do not realize that my heritage rests with that country. I am glad that they feel free to talk honestly with me, but they do not recognize how difficult it is for me to keep my silence at times.

It seems that the major concern that people are having is that the German

137

population is not accepting the American language (which is considered to be English) and is not adapting to the American culture and American values with enough speed. They are concerned that the Germans are motivated to change the American society into a copy of Germany, rather than adapting to our ways. When they speak with me I hear their curiosity and their fear. Fear that the 'American' way of life will be overcome by the 'German' way of life. Recently I am also detecting fear that some Germans may be conspiring with the German forces to gain control of our world. This has lately begun to evolve into anger. Fear is easily transformed into anger. Anger is more comfortable an emotion than the uncertainty of fear and intense fear expressed as anger is a frightening thing. I am worried about where this will take us.

****

This spring the anti-German sentiment rose proportionately to the drastic increase in American casualties of the war. In May our Governor ordered that the English language was to be the language of instruction in public and private schools, and of all conversations on trains, on phones, in all public places and all sermons in churches.

Out of the six German speaking congregations in Muscatine, Aunt Anna was a member of Zion Lutheran that was founded by German immigrants in 1885. Zion also operated a school which conducted its instruction in German.

Aunt Anna never had any thought of leaving that church because of her fondness for the Pastor, John Haefner. "At times I cannot wait for the Sunday sermon because of the insight of Pastor Haefner," said Aunt Anna. "He makes the lessons of the bible come to life right here in Muscatine. We often have sermons in German in the morning and English in the evening. I like to attend them both because the meanings that I find in the words and phrases in German at times vary from English interpretations. Attending both also gives me a chance to socialize with my German friends and my English speaking friends in the coffee gatherings that often occur afterwards. It keeps me in touch."

****

In January a group of businessmen began to meet regularly at the Hotel Muscatine. On several occasions the group discussed the loyalty of various community members. At one of the meetings it was determined that Pastor Haefner did not fly an American flag at his home and that a committee should be designated to present him with a flag and ask him to fly it. (http://www.elca.org/JLE/Articles?697 , Reverend Paul Ostrem, "Loyalty Days")

Reverend John Haefner

A group formed and marched ceremoniously to the reverend's home, picking up members along the way. By the time they had paraded through the downtown and reached the pastor's residence, three to four hundred people had gathered.

(http://www.elca.org/JLE/Articles?697 , Reverend Paul Ostrem, "Loyalty Days")

Reverend Haefner opened the door and listened to the speech that had been prepared to accompany the flag. When he agreed to fly the flag and to keep it flying at his residence the group was satisfied and dispersed. (http://www.elca.org/JLE/Articles?697 , Reverend Paul Ostrem, "Loyalty Days")

This would seem to be the end of the matter but it was, in reality, only the beginning. The event became a catalyst for the opening up of what seemed to some to be the festering German problem in the community. The next day one of the local papers published a letter which stated that "it comes as a warning to those residents of the community not in sympathy with the government or the present war," and which "calls attention to the fact that the community will no longer tolerate disloyalty". A letter in the competing paper said that "I think it wise to call the attention of Mr. Haefner and of others who feel the same as he does, to the fact that the community has stood for all the disloyalty that it will stand for and that it would be the part of wisdom on their part to be very careful that they give no further cause for complaint".

(http://www.elca.org/JLE/Articles?697 , Reverend Paul Ostrem, "Loyalty Days")

It was a long and dreadful year. I felt no joy when victory over Germany was finally declared in November. Others may have a sense of elation but I cannot help but focus on the damage that has been done to the relations in this community. Will the German-Americans ever be trusted as true Iowans and will the German-Americans ever trust their fellow Iowans again? There are times when a major positive result does not erase the internal damaging consequences.

I lashed on my snow boots and trudged to the Indian mounds through deep drifts. Thick fallen branches covered the hill. I brushed off the snow, sat and contemplated the mighty Mississippi which was blended into the horizon by a thick steam that rose over its surface. I have noticed this occur on the river at other times. It seems as though the river is simmering beneath its icy lid. It is becoming hotter and hotter and soon will come to a boil.

****

It was with great sadness that I watched Cornelius leave to take a job as a salesperson of Edison phonographs in Des Moines. It is so far away and I am not certain that he will be able to contain his emotions in that setting, without any family support. He was in quite a state over the world war activity and his desire to participate but I think reality has returned to him. He has calmed considerably. It is true that my business can no longer support him and that he has not proven himself capable of sustaining a store in the town.

It could be that it is time for him to move away from the home of his mother and father and to try to function on his own. It might actually prove to be advantageous for him to be in charge of his own life and his own time. I am not certain, however, how well Harriet will function without him near. For that matter, I am not certain how I will function without him near. His wry sense of humor has always been such a source of relief for me. No matter how difficult things seem, a few minutes with Cornelius puts things in perspective.

Shortly after Cornelius left for Des Moines, I was sitting in my Cadillac outside of the hospital following a medical appointment. A drunk driver came swerving down the street and careened off of my car, plunged across the hospital lawn and slowed when it grazed the side of the medical building. Several nurses and a patient saved their lives by leaping off of the lawn swing as the vehicle sped past. My chauffer ran across the lawn in chase, jumped into the vehicle and brought it to a stop. He grabbed the key to the battery box and prevented the driver from departing until the police arrived. (The Muscatine Journal, July 12, 1918, pg 7, "Hold Farmer in Auto Accident")

The world seems to be sinking into a pit of misery, distrust and irresponsibility. Throughout all of this, my business continues to decline while that of my competitor profits. At least I will not have to continue to observe him being lauded for the victories of the ball teams. That man accepts credit for everything. You would think that it was him, and not the young athletes, that was putting forth all of the effort for the games. Foot traffic in his store will now decline because you will not have all of the ball team followers checking with him about the prospects for the next game. His business will sink to the low level that it merits. Although it is difficult to find anything positive about a world war accompanied by a draft, perhaps this is the exception.

Elsie

Aunt Anna's heart was broken. When the papers reflected anti-German sentiment, she took it personally but after her observation of the pain and sorrow of her Reverend Haefner she sits and pets Sugar and cries silently. I have often thought during this past year that little Sugar was a gift from God for Aunt Anna. When Anna takes a seat, Sugar jumps up into her lap and snuggles against her rather ample middle. I think that the dog senses her sorrow and attempts to comfort her.

She was very upset when the Governor ordered that the sermons could not occur in German because she was aware that many of the newer immigrants could not speak English or at least could not communicate in the language well enough to comprehend the sermons. The government's response was that such people should worship in their own homes.

"How were they supposed to do that, Elsie?" asked Aunt Anna. "They could pray in their own homes but how could they hear the sermon and participate in communion and the various religious sacraments? Even if they were able, does the government not understand that an important element of church is being part of a family, of belonging to a religious community? How are these people going to experience the sense of belonging in a time of war against their country of origin, a time when they need the religious community the most?"

She was of the opinion that her beloved Reverend Haefner had become the whipping post for the anti-German and anti-immigration segment of the community. All of the anger and suspicion in Muscatine was being focused upon him. Any statement or action that he took was misrepresented and magnified by that group of people.

An editorial in the local paper on January 3rd commented on a remark that the minister had made indicating his perception that there was prejudice against him in the community. It said that the "prejudice is entirely of his own making... Had he merely given a casual aid to the various projects which have

145

engrossed our attention since the outbreak of the war he would have aided greatly in the work of cementing friendships among all Americans and of erasing suspicion from our community life". It suggested that "it took a visit of a committee from the community to pry loose information as to patriotic activities, the knowledge of which a loyal American citizen should be proud to proclaim to the world" and ended by stating that, "Mr. Haefner and men who, like him, are looked up to by an element among our foreign born population can contribute mightily to that national solidarity which alone can hasten the victorious end of the war". (http://www.elca.org/JLE/Articles?697 , Reverend Paul Ostrem, "Loyalty Days") The implication clearly was that Pastor Haefner's loyalty to our war effort was dubious.

After the school board voted to discontinue the teaching of German in the public schools in April, the teaching of German in the parochial schools became a target of concern. A group of 'concerned citizens' drafted a resolution calling for all schools in the community to end the practice of conducting lessons in German. The group then presented their resolution to the leaders of the German institutions in the community, one of which was led by the Reverend Haefner. As a result the Zion Church Council recommended that German no longer be used in its parochial school, and the congregation gave a unanimous standing agreement to its implementation, with no dissenting votes. (http://www.elca.org/JLE/Articles?697 , Reverend Paul Ostrem, "Loyalty Days")

The following Sunday I accompanied Aunt Anna to her church to personally witness the words of the verbally gifted minister and the response of the congregation.

We slipped into one of the few remaining pews as many of the congregation whispered greetings in a mix of German and English and continued to murmur excitedly until the young minister appeared. He was a thin man of medium height with brown hair and eyes, who would have normally blended unnoticed into the crowd.

The congregation quieted as he walked down the aisle and took his place in the front of the room. After several hymns, all listened intently as the service began. Reverend Haefner asked for his members to be "of stout heart" in his Sunday sermon and he urged them to trust in the Lord. "Giving up the German language in our schools is a severe sacrifice. In fact it almost becomes to us an affliction. We have always cherished the German language because of its associations with incidents in our early lives which are clear to us. It has been the mother tongue, the agency through which we gave expression to our heart throbs in childhood. It is hard to give up the language which we learned at our mother's knee but we do it with stout heart because we are asked to dissolve our differences and become one." (http://www.elca.org/JLE/Articles?697 , Reverend Paul Ostrem, "Loyalty Days")

When we arrived home and Aunt Anna and I sat in the kitchen and consumed tea along with her homemade cookies, she asked, "Well, Elsie, what do you think of my Reverend Haefner? Isn't he the best speaker that you have ever heard?"

"You are so right, Aunt Anna. I do not think that I will ever forget the words that he preached today. He seems to be able to get to the very heart of things."

"Surely they will leave him in peace now, don't you agree, Elsie? He has done everything that he has been asked."

"I am certain that they will move on to another target, Aunt Anna. The good minister has dealt with a difficult situation very well, in my view."

"I can't stand it when they pick on him, Elsie. He has done so much for so many of us in the congregation during our times of need."

A few days later, I read in the newspaper that Reverend Haefner stated that although the teaching of German would be eliminated from the school, opening exercises would still be conducted in German and a German hymn would be sung followed by a reading from the German Bible. He also said that his church "reserves the right to use the language for religious devotion. (http://www.elca.org/JLE/Articles?697 , Reverend Paul Ostrem, "Loyalty Days")

"Good Lord, Reverend Haefner, this is not going to end well," I said aloud.

Aunt Anna, who was standing behind me said, "What, Elsie? Is there trouble of some type?"

"Aunt Anna," I responded, "you better prepare yourself for future problems with your good minister. He is not the kind of man who can just nod politely and shut up. He clearly views himself as one of God's shepherds instead of one of his sheep. What he is saying is going to appear to be defiant to the "concerned citizens" group. They will not let this stand."

Aunt Anna retired to her bedroom and did not come out at dinner time or in the evening. When she did not appear for her usual morning baking session, I went to her room to talk to her. Her eyes were swollen and red from her constant tears. "Staying in your bedroom will not help Reverend Haefner, Aunt Anna. This is just going to depress you even further."

"I cannot stand what that man is enduring, Elsie. This is so wrong for him

147

and his family," she responded. "I just don't have the energy to get out of bed. Let me stay here alone."

I went to the phone and called the reverend and informed him of Aunt Anna's misery. I asked if he could possibly take some time out of his day to come and speak with her. Perhaps the ability to express her sympathy to him will help her improve. He said he would be over in a couple of hours.

I returned to Aunt Anna's room and informed her that she better get up and get dressed because the good minister was going to come for a visit. The color immediately flowed back into her face. She said, "Oh my goodness, Elsie, I must make certain that we have a good piece of cake to serve him and maybe some cookies to take home to his family." She jumped out of bed, got dressed and spent the remaining time in the kitchen and dining room, readying the area for her honored guest.

When Reverend Haefner arrived Aunt Anna greeted him at the door and escorted him into the dining room where the table was loaded with such a display of cookies, candies, cakes and pies that the reverend asked if any other people were expected. I laughed and told him that this was all for him.

Aunt Anna made certain that he was comfortably seated and supplied with coffee, cream and sugar, a glass of water, a tumbler of orange juice and anything else that he might possibly need. She began by expressing to him, her sorrow over all that had occurred. She told him how much she anticipated his sermons and that she spent much of her time thinking over the lessons that he presented.

He thanked her for her kind regards. He said, "Dear Anna, you do not need to worry about me. I am much stronger than I appear." He told her that he had been born in Beikheim, Bavaria, Germany as one of seven children. He had grown to have some toughness being a member of such a large family. The traditional trade of his family was blacksmithing and the making of armor. His older brother took over the ancestral business and he was left to pursue his own area of interest. He came to the United States in 1889 at the age of 14 and was able to find work on a farm. Eventually, with the financial assistance of the Iowa Lutheran Synod, he graduated from the seminary. He obtained his citizenship in 1896 after completing the process in the shortest amount of time allowed by the law. ("Dennoch" Muscatine, Iowa : Paul D. Ostrem, 2002.)

He concluded by assuring Aunt Anna that he had been through a great deal to get here and that he was not going away. He felt that God had led him to this avocation and to this community and to this conflict. He said that he was thoroughly prepared for this and that she need not worry. He made her promise that he was welcome to stop by for cookies and cake if there was ever a time when he felt down in the dumps. She, of course, agreed and he said that, with her support, he and his family can handle this. He emphasized that Aunt Anna is now part of their team.

After the reverend left, Aunt Anna simply glowed. She said that she intended to bake and deliver cakes, cookies and candies to the parsonage every week. She thought that a little sugar would do nothing but help the situation and added that it was the least that she could do now that she was a part of the team. I laughed and advised her to not let the Kautz bakery know that she is basically going into the business.

George

On June 14th, Flag Day, I was working with my father dusting and polishing the watches in the case at the front of the store. The growing noise of a gathering crowd drew our attention as we noticed people rushing down the street in what appeared to be a state of panic. Father and I stepped outside and asked a man if he knew what was going on. He said that he had heard that there was going to be a marching of that German traitor, the Minister Haefner, down the street to city hall for desecrating our great American flag.

"My God, George," said my father. "Can this really be happening?"

"Dad, I don't know. Let us just watch what is going on."

The sounds of the crowd became louder and rowdier, and we saw a phalanx of men round the corner and proceed down the street in a growing throng. Marchers carried signs which read "German instruction means English destruction", "100 percent Americanism breeds confidence. Disloyalty breeds disturbance", "Mr. Bond Slacker, You're next", "Watchful waiting wins the War" and "We are taking the 'Germ' out of German". The marchers were yelling and cheering with red faces and riotous enthusiasm. People gathering on the curb were greeting them with hisses and boos.

"Are they hissing and booing 'at' this demonstration or 'for' this demonstration, George? I cannot know."

"I am not certain, Dad. I don't understand what this is all about," I replied.

At that point the marching horde parted and we saw that the Reverend Haefner with his head bowed was being paraded behind a man who carried the American flag and beside a man who carried his hat. A sign was attached with a cord to the reverend's back which read "If you don't like to speak the English language use signs". On his front was attached a sign that read, "In the future I promise to be a good American".

(http://www.elca.org/JLE/Articles?697 , Reverend Paul Ostrem, "Loyalty Days")

As the throng passed by the mass of spectators that had gathered on the streets, many hooted and cried out "We won't hurt you - watch your step!" I was surprised to notice that banners were carried in the parade by prominent professional and business men, but I was shocked to see that several prominent ministers also participated.

Members of Zion Lutheran Church quietly observed the humiliation of the pastor with tears streaming down their cheeks. Some of them ran along the parade on the sidewalk in an attempt to show Reverend Haefner their support. Many of my customers were participants in the parade and waved at my father and myself as they marched past.

How strange that they are expressing this anti-German sentiment and also greeting my father, an immigrant from Germany, in such a friendly fashion. They clearly possess no animosity toward German immigrants when they know them and trust them. This seems to be a result of the fear that accompanies a world war.

As my father saw the minister he said, "George, I have to go and stop this. The reverend is a good man. We cannot just stand and watch this. This is wrong."

I grabbed his arm to prevent him from proceeding forward and said, "Dad, you can't obstruct it. You can't run out there at this point. It is too dangerous. You speak with a German accent; you can't afford to draw attention to yourself.

I watched as tears flowed down his face. "Dad, wipe your tears. Don't let anybody see you cry about this. Go and lock up the store and we will follow the crowd to city hall to see what happens."

"I cannot watch and do nothing to defend this man, George," said my father.

"Then you need to stay in the store and take care of business while I follow the mob," I replied. "Wait here for my return. I will tell you all that I see."

I ran to catch up to the parade as they reached City Hall. About one thousand people had gathered around a local physician, Dr. Oliver, on the lawn. "It is the usual custom in instances and demonstrations of this sort to present the culprit with an American flag. In this case we are not going to do this as the flag has suffered enough disrespect in the hands of Reverend Haefner. I am not speaking hearsay but from what I have seen myself. It is also a custom to make the disloyal kneel and kiss the flag but we think that the flag has suffered sufficient humiliation," pronounced the Doctor. Looking dramatically at the reverend he warned, "We want you to know that the Hindenburg line is broken in Iowa and especially in Muscatine. If you do not believe that this is your country and our flag is your flag you had better go back to Germany and the sooner the better. There is not a person in Muscatine that would be glad to see you go. However, while you are a citizen of the United States you are going to respect the American flag - if we are compelled to make you. This is only a warning to you. Let it be a lesson to every pro-German that might be in Muscatine. If there should ever be a 'next time' all I can say to you is that we cannot promise to handle you so gently." After the rally, the minister was escorted to his car and allowed to depart. ("Dennoch" Muscatine, Iowa : Paul D. Ostrem, 2002.)

I noticed the owner of a local business, who was also of German descent, standing silently at the edge of the crowd. I made my way to him and asked, "What in the world are we Germans doing here?"

"We clearly have no sense," he replied.

"Do you have any idea how this happened?" I asked. He said that it is reported that the minister disrespected the flag.

When he was at a regularly scheduled meeting of businessmen at the Muscatine Hotel, the speaker for the day was a former member of the German navy who had also served in the United States infantry and had fought in the Spanish-American War. The speaker described his personal observations of the horrific behaviors of the Prussian army with passion. He ended his oration by saying "You ought to pity those men of German origin in this time of crisis who despite their natural love for the old land are loyal to the core as Americans but you must insist that those who have accepted the benefits and privileges of American citizenship live up to their responsibilities. There is no disgrace equal to that of those who stand convicted as perjurers by forgetting the oath when they foreswore all other allegiance and declared their loyalty to the American government, the American flag and the American institutions...Why in the name of God don't they now stand by the country that welcomed them?"

A group then drove to Pastor Haefner's parsonage and asked that he accompany them. The reverend waited for about an hour in the car while some gathered around it called out "Throw him in the river", "Get a rail," and "Tar and feathers". ("Dennoch" Muscatine, Iowa : Paul D. Ostrem, 2002.)

Meanwhile in the meeting, the Home Guard Band magically appeared and played several patriotic tunes, after which Dr. A.J. Oliver said to the crowd, "Ladies and Gentlemen: my father served four years in the army and my grandfather went through the entire civil war. The flag we hold so dear was fought for by them and I'll be damned if I can stand by quietly and see it insulted and dragged in the mud by a cowardly pro-German. This is the treatment that the flag in the possession of Reverend Haefner has been subjected to. We now intend to take Reverend Haefner and dress him in a manner best fitted to him and show him to the citizens of Muscatine by marching him through the streets. We have asked that no violence be done to Reverend Haefner and have pledged him our word that we will return him safe and uninjured to his family." ("Dennoch" Muscatine, Iowa : Paul D. Ostrem, 2002.)

When the reverend was removed from the car he tried to speak but was silenced by the derision of the crowd and a command barked by Dr. Oliver. He was seized and restrained. A member of the throng took the man's hat from him and tied signs around his body. Home-made signs had been prepared and were handed out to the crowd and they began their march of humiliation up and down the streets of the downtown business district. ("Dennoch" Muscatine, Iowa : Paul D. Ostrem, 2002.)

****

My head was spinning as I walked back to the store. "Dad," I said, "I think it is time to lock up for the day and go home. You, Mom, Helen and I need to sit down and discuss the things that have occurred here today." I called Helen and told her that we were headed home and that a lot of things had happened downtown today that we all need to talk about. I asked her to please make sure Mom was present, put on a pot of coffee and send home any neighbors or friends that might be visiting.

As we all sat soberly around the kitchen table I related the events of the day. My father reacted with anger, Helen with sadness and my mother with fear. "Are they going to come and get us, George? Are they going to parade us down the streets? We try to speak English but no matter how hard we try, we still seem to sound German. I don't think we even have a flag. Do we need to get a flag?"

"Mom, you and Dad are under no threat of harm. In fact, I do not believe that anybody in our family needs to fear. Through your years of operating a saloon and my years of operating a store in the community, the people of this town have gotten to know us well and they have found that we can be trusted. Nobody will doubt our patriotism. We all know that the majority of people in this town are loving neighbors and responsible citizens.

"People are vulnerable when they are fearful. At this time, and rightly so, they are terrified of Germany and the impact that Germany might have on their lives. They are very susceptible to the fanning of those fears at such a time. There are those out there who are attempting to inflame emotions in this volatile atmosphere."

"Why in the world would they want to do that?" asked Helen.

"That is hard to determine," I responded. "Some people are so fearful that they seem to not be able to help the constant expression of their every concern. They see a statement that a suspicious person makes or an action that occurs and they attribute all sorts of intent and motivation, most of which is made up out of their own heads.

"I have always believed that there are also people out there of just plain evil intent. A small portion of the populace exists with a great deal of misery and hatred in their hearts. It could be born in them or it could be because of the travails of life. They live in misery and see a world full of happy and loving people outside of their doors. They are not able to get through the portal to the other side of the door and they therefore attempt to make those cheery people out there come into their world of hatred and misery. They will use anything to spread their hatred.

"Whatever comes to public attention is a potential target. Right now the war with Germany makes our population a perfect foil for these people to focus their hatreds and to attempt to increase the negative emotions of others toward us.

"The people in this community know that you are good Americans. You are well trusted because people are knowledgeable about you due to your participation in the business community. You need to keep their trust. As an American who speaks broken English that sounds primarily like German, you can do a lot of good in this community. People will have faith in what you say and your behavior informs them that the new immigrants are loyal and trustworthy.

"This will not last. Once this war is over, and hopefully it will be soon, our life in Muscatine will go back to normal. The fear of the population will lesson. The sense of justice and respect that we have experienced for so many years in this little town will return."

When we were in bed that evening Helen said, "Have I told you how much I love you, George?"

"What brings on the accolades?" I asked.

154

"You are so sensible and so wise. Your positive outlook always causes you to see the best in people. I feel that I am totally safe with you in my life and that we will weather any storm."

"That is because we will, Helen," I replied.

****

The May newspaper indicated that Dr. Oliver had filed charges in court against Reverend Haefner on the charge of desecration of the flag. I attended as much of the trial as I was able. It was clear that Pastor Haefner's flag had been allowed to fall on the ground but it was not possible to ascertain exactly how it arrived in that location. It could have been blown down by the weather. It could have been a faulty flag holder. It was also indicated that one of the pastor's daughters had been playing parade with the flag and had been marching around with it and perhaps did not place it properly back into its location.

What is certain is that Dr. Oliver testified that several people had called him to inform him that the minister's flag was lying on the ground. He said that, "At about 10 o'clock I started for the home. I picked up a friend and the two of us proceeded to the place. We found the flag lying in the flower garden off the porch. My friend picked it up and when Reverend Haefner came to the door, asked him if he was aware that the flag had been lying in the mud. He declared that he was not. He then picked up the flag and took it into the house without further words." The jury found Reverend Haefner to be not guilty. ("Dennoch" Muscatine, Iowa : Paul D. Ostrem, 2002.) It was clear that he had not intended to desecrate the flag. Such a big ruckus about so little. Eventually the noise about the reverend lessened and the public focus shifted.

****

Local concern about Germans took a precipitous drop in November with the declaration of victory in the war. My family and friends gathered and celebrated well into the night.

My mother cried at the news of the war victory. She said, "I am so glad to be in America, George. Maybe now we can become a real part of the community, even though we are German immigrants."

"Mom, you and Dad are real Americans in every sense of the word. America is defined by the people who came first. It is also defined by the people that came thereafter. Immigration is an essential element to the definition of the country. Read what it says on the statue of liberty plaque:

"Keep, ancient lands, your storied pomp!" cries she
With silent lips. "Give me your tired, your poor,
Your huddled masses yearning to breathe free,
The wretched refuse of your teeming shore.
Send these, the homeless, tempest-tossed to me,
I lift my lamp beside the golden door!"

My parents are the real America. I always knew that to be true but now they also, are certain. It took weeks for us all to wipe the smiles off of our faces. The negativity is now history. Goodness prevailed. All is right with the world. I just knew this is how it would all turn out.

Chapter 9: 1919
Fitch

Some of my investments are not paying off. I had expected for the oil field investments in particular to have yielded rewards by this point in time. (The Muscatine Journal, August 2, 1921, pg 1 "CITY SHOCKED GEORGE VOLGER SLAIN BY F.W. SWAN; LATTER THEN KILLS SELF; ACT PLANNED") This leaves me without the comfort of an adequate cushion of savings. However, I have opened an optical branch in my store that promises to be a profitable endeavor which can compensate for some of my losses. Eyeglasses will become a more central issue in life as people are living longer and as books become more available. The public is becoming very aware of the difference that a pair of well made eyeglasses can create in every day living. It is rather costly to set up for this new specialization but I believe that it will be worth it.

****

Prohibition will become reality in Muscatine this year, although the rules regarding alcohol have changed on a rather constant basis in Iowa throughout the years. I don't mind having a drink or two if the situation warrants but I really have never been much of a drinker. I think prohibition may be a good thing for my business because instead of customers drinking all of their money away in the saloons, they are more likely to have the funds for jewelry and watches.

Of course, Elsie is a bit out of her mind about the subject. She is certain that alcohol will cause the end of civilization as we know it. As a member of the Women's Temperance cause, she has forever been sitting around with her sister Temperance supporters and hatching one plot after another to cause this evil to disappear from human kind. Lately they have been joining forces with the suffragettes based on the premise that if women get the vote, they will vote in droves for temperance.

Not even that goofy little animal, Sugar, is able to divert her focus. I was in disbelief when she brought that constantly urinating, shedding little beast into our home. Even Aunt Anna, with all of her German focus on tidiness and order, has allowed the dog to climb all over the furniture and perch on the back of the settee. She actually has this animal sleep with her in bed and is in the process of crocheting a sweater for her so she will not be cold this winter.

It is not possible for me to comprehend what positives this dog is bringing into their lives.

Elsie refers to her as 'my sweet baby girl'. She and Aunt Anna continue to tell her that they love her and pet her all of the time. The dog particularly likes to lick people and forever licks their hands and arms and even their faces, if they fail to protect themselves adequately.

I have pointed out to both of them that dogs consume anything they see on the ground, are full of germs, and even use their tongues to clean their private parts. Surely they cannot think that allowing the animal to salivate all over their bodies is a good idea?

They just laugh at me and say that I need to 'feel the love'.

I do not understand of what they are talking. This is not a human. This is an animal and this animal is not capable of feeling and returning the human 'love' of which they speak. I cannot stand it when I see them attributing human emotions to this beast.

Elsie

I am glad that prohibition is finally in full effect in this country. The community has some responsibility to place barriers between a family's paycheck and the profits of the saloon owner. I hate to think of all of the bread that has been taken out of the mouths of innocent children by the bar owners' practice of pushing alcohol onto irresponsible customers. Saloon owners make more money when they sell more alcohol and there is a constant effort to increase the alcohol consumption of their customers. This prohibition is a well-deserved line of defense that has been given to mothers.

I am aware that there are many in the community who are against this action, in particular, George Volger. He stopped me on the street the other day and said that he had heard that I am helping the prohibition people organize their efforts on the local level. He said that he was quite surprised by this since I am familiar with his parents and know that they are not evil in any way. George seemed quite annoyed. I told him that we will just need to have a disagreement on this issue because his life experiences with alcohol have differed greatly from my own.

Most of these people who favor the legality of alcohol have either benefitted from the profits of alcohol consumption or have not personally experienced the consequences of alcohol use and are not aware that intoxication causes many men to forget about their families and their responsibilities. They have not endured the single mother problem. There is no way for a woman to consistently feed her family without the support of a man in this society at this time. If 'Daddy' does not come home with the paycheck, what is 'Mommy' to do? She can go begging to other family members for just so long.

Families are dependent on the common sense of the man of the house and this is often the area where family breakdown begins. Young ladies need to put more thought into the character of the men that they marry. He may be handsome and charming and he may dance well, but all of this lessens in importance after marriage, if he has faulty reasoning. Lack of wisdom results in intoxication, in bankruptcy, in violence.

I certainly thought of all of those things when I decided to marry Fitch. Of course I had my share of young men who displayed interest in developing a relationship with me. I chose instead to opt for a proven commodity.

****

It bothers me to observe how distressed Fitch has become over the success that George has experienced in the community. He may have a nice store with a pretty clock outside and a streetlight and a fountain but he can never have the respect and prominence of Fitch. Many boards and organizations depend on Fitch to be a part of their concerns and to provide personal counsel. Fitch's years of experience with the public accounts for something. I think that he is worrying needlessly.

I wish he could take some pleasure in the presence of little Sugar. It might relieve some of his misery to experience the companionship that a dog can provide but he seems to be unable to obtain anything positive from the animal. Instead, he is spending more and more time staring at the river while he sits on the Indian mounds at the park. He goes there when it is hot, in the rain and in the snow and remains late into the evening hours. I am worried about him.

****

Although it is difficult to think about, I have noticed a great decline in Fitch's sexual appetite, at least when it comes to me. He often remains in the living room and reads late into the evening. Brushing my hair into a shine and donning an appealing night gown and a wonderfully scented perfume is of no avail because by the time he comes upstairs to bed, I am sound asleep.

I do not know how to approach this issue with him or with anybody else for that matter. We are taught that women are not supposed to have sexual desires themselves, but my primary need is to bear a child. I can't figure out any other way to accomplish this feat.

After much contemplation I decided to go to Dr. Braunwarth for a discussion of the situation. I am so grateful that I have a female doctor with whom I am able to discuss these issues. I would never, ever be able to mention them to the common male doctor. I couldn't decide if it would be better to approach Dr. Sarah or Emma and figured I would let chance decide and talk with whichever doctor is available when I arrive.

After the nurse seated me comfortably in the examining room, Dr. Sarah entered and sat at the desk. "What seems to be the problem today, Elsie?"

"I am a little uncomfortable discussing this issue with you, Dr. Sarah. I don't think that it is a proper conversation for two ladies to have," I replied.

"Let me assure you, Elsie that I have heard and seen just about anything that you can imagine and probably a great many things that you cannot. I know you have had a desire to have a child for quite some time and I assume that your problem has something to do with that. I have delivered so many babies and have dealt with every aspect of procreation and sexuality for years. Don't bother yourself with worrying about 'proper' or 'improper' topics with me. In fact it is usually the so called 'improper' problems in life that would benefit by the most discussion."

"I will get straight to it then, Dr. Sarah. Fitch does not seem to be interested in me sexually any longer. I have tried everything but nothing seems to have an impact. I don't know if I am doing something wrong or if something is the matter with me. You are right that I desperately want to have a child but I can never see that happening in this circumstance."

"Elsie, you have told me repeatedly how stressed out and unhappy your husband has become over time. That sort of feeling can drain a man of all of his energy and can greatly lesson his appetites. Are you still seeing this downward spiral happening with him?"

"Yes, I am. Everything seems to be going wrong as far as he is concerned. He has lost faith in humanity and I cannot emphasize enough how it all seems to focus on George Volger in his mind. George seems to have the type of personality that attracts everybody in town and his business is prospering proportionately. Fitch thinks that his years of experience should give him a priority position with the community and particularly with jewelry customers. It doesn't seem to be working that way."

"I think that you need to understand the impact that his negativity most likely has on his sexual behaviors," said Doctor Sarah. "This is a very common consequence of distress. I doubt that it has anything to do with you at all."

"Maybe I should discuss it with him, Doctor Sarah. Do you think I should bring it up after dinner and let him know that I understand his situation?"

"I really don't think that is a good idea," she responded. "I am wondering if he has sensed your ongoing drive to have a baby. This may feel like another failure to him and he may worry about his ability to perform the proper male role in your relationship. You do not want him to feel additional pressure. Give it some time, Elsie and give him a chance to heal from his present sorrows."

****

David and I take our dogs for walks several times a week. I cannot stand to keep Sugar from the company of her mother for more than a few days in a row. She leaps and pants excitedly when she sees Cookie coming up the walk. On days when we stay home, she lies by the front door and cries. I know what it is like to miss a mother. I can't stand doing that to her.

Sometimes we walk through the city park that is across the street from my home. I prefer walking on the shore of the river. Fitch likes to view the river while looking down from the Indian mounds but I like being close enough to observe all of the life that exists within its banks.

The best place for such a walk is the downtown riverfront. The area where the businesses are located and where the clammers work is kept relatively clear of brush and I can sit on a stone or a fallen branch near its banks and watch the turtles and frogs and the occasional muskrat, foraging along the shore. Herons stand on the rocks on one of their incredibly long legs, with the other tucked up under their bottoms and scan the terrain. I am not certain what they are always in search of. Perhaps as with most people, they also are not aware.

I find it somewhat humorous that the eagles remind me of Fitch. They primarily visit the area in the winter time and can be identified by their little white heads attached to a huge wing span. They mostly make their presence known as small dots soaring far up in the sky or perching on the very top of the tallest tree. They watch us suspiciously from afar and seem to know better than to come down from the sky and mingle with we earth bound creatures. They have a majestic look about them and appear to possess some fundamental wisdom and understanding, but their lonely perch does not appear to yield happiness or joy.

As David and I were strolling along he indicated that he had brought me a surprise. I said, "David, I have access to many times the funds that you do. Please do not be buying me any presents. I just don't need it."

He laughed and pulled a bottle of whiskey from his jacket. "What is that?" I asked him.

162

"It is whisky, Elsie. I thought we would toast the passage of temperance."

"Where did you get that? It is illegal for you to have that," I said.

"Bootleggers are everywhere, Elsie. I think that there are more people selling alcohol now than there were before prohibition."

"Put that away, David. I am most certainly not going to stand here and guzzle alcohol from a bottle with you. Just who exactly do you think you are dealing with?"

"I know who I am dealing with, Elsie. A sweet, wonderful, charming and if you don't mind my saying so, sexy young lady."

"Stop it, David. I do mind you saying so. You are not treating me with respect."

"Relax, everything is okay. I know that you are attracted to me. There is nothing wrong with you and I having a little fun. I don't mean to be disrespectful."

"I do find you to be an attractive young man, David and I do enjoy the time that I spend with you but you need to understand that this is a friendship and that is all it is. My marriage is very important to me. I have made a promise to Fitch that I will be there for him, through sickness and health and for better or worse. I take that seriously. I know that he would be there for me also. Now let this be the end of this. I do not want you to speak to me of this again."

"Okay, Elsie, I am sorry. I will behave myself. This doesn't mean that you will stop taking walks with Cookie and me does it?"

His mournful expression made me laugh and I responded, "How could I discontinue our walks? Sugar would pack her bags and run away from home to return to her mother at your house."

As we continued on our way, David dropped the bottle of whiskey into the rocks by the river. "I think I have just made some future fisherman very happy," he mused.

George

Prohibition finally passed on a national basis although it has been erratically in practice in Iowa for some time. My father died on March 2nd, after an illness and although my heart breaks at his loss, I am thankful that he had little awareness of the final achievement of Carrie Nation. How fortunate we are that he closed his saloon several years ago and that he will feel no impact of this national decision.

I find it hard to understand where the country is going with this. Having grown up assisting my father in the saloon, I believe I have an understanding of the impact of alcohol. I believe that it is not the substance that causes the problems in judgment but that it is the problems in judgment that cause the difficulties with alcohol. I have observed how the vast majority of men are able to be exposed to this substance with no negative consequence.

I do not think that this prohibition will last. After time, the American people will see the nonsense in this law. The final victory will be that of my father. He will be watching this all come to pass from his comfortable home in heaven.

****

My business continues to flourish. Mr. Swan, however, had another auction in May which may be an indication that regular business practices are not proving sufficiently profitable for him. The auction has become a recurring strategy for him. I do not think that the community really believes that he has this quantity of inventory in his store. Clearly he is bringing in lower quality items to auction off. It is meant to seem like a big sale to the customer but it is nothing of the kind. Although I believe in aggressive and creative marketing, I have a problem with misrepresentation to the public and dishonest practices.

I saw him on the street the other day and was shocked by his changed appearance. His hair is whiter and he appears to be rather stooped over and unsteady. He did not seem to see me and when I said, "Hi, Mr. Swan," he did not look in my direction nor respond. Perhaps he did not notice me.

****

What he needs to concern himself about is the behaviors of Elsie. As Helen and I were sitting out on the porch last Sunday, several people stopped by to mention that they had observed Elsie and David Porter walking their dogs around the community. It has become the 'talk of the town' and I cannot see how Mr. Swan can ignore it. If he has not seen them himself, he needs new glasses. Perhaps he needs to stop buying them at his own store and go to a real place of business.

I asked Helen if she still thought that I should just mind my own business now that this has become public knowledge. She said that "Often people do not see things that are right in front of them because they do not want to see them. Maybe Mr. Swan does not want to see this and does not want to have to deal with it. He probably knows the best action to take regarding this, in his own world.

"Another way to view this situation, George, is that Mr. Swan would most likely be having a fit about this if he thought that there was any reason for concern. Most likely he is certain that he need not worry about Elsie's relationship with this man. He probably knows that the only affection that they share is that involving canines."

Chapter 10: 1920
Fitch:

At times it is difficult to go on. I no longer pray to God because God does not care about me. I go to the Indian mounds to talk to Mollie. If there is a heaven my Mollie is certain to be there and Mollie always heard what I had to say. Never once did she find my concerns to be unimportant or insignificant. My Mollie must be watching over me.

I sense that we communicate through the bird songs. When I have a question, I watch for an eagle to dip a wing in response to my thoughts. Vultures circling above the river forewarn of Mollie's fears about my future. There seem to be no cheery little wrens or busybody goldfinches entering into the space of my contemplations. The hummingbirds and meadowlarks are long gone from my soul. Maybe this is a message that I have stayed too long on this earth. I appear to no longer have a positive purpose here. Perhaps Mollie is calling me home.

I do not speak to Elsie about these things. She is such an optimistic young woman. I cannot figure out how the 'world is a wonderful place' and 'all will work out for the best' have become her life mottos. If it were not for Aunt Anna, she might not have even survived her childhood and without my resources and support, she would have a hard time making it in this world.

****

I find it hard to get out of bed in the mornings and I am experiencing a lot of pain in my back. I continue to drag myself to the store each day, in the hopes of making a few dollars. I must earn enough money to pay the bills and I am finding it increasingly difficult. My investment in the oil fields proved to be a total fiasco and by virtue of that and all of my other asinine investments, I have managed to lose my entire emergency financial cushion.

Because of all of this general malaise, I had decided to let the holidays pass without the usual extensive efforts at the store. Much to my surprise Elsie informed me that she and Aunt Anna planned on being my 'holiday workers'. She reported that they would be the 'little elves' that help the 'big Santa'. I guess that means me.

The next week she and Aunt Anna came and decorated everything that could not move away from their reach. Anna brought holiday cookies and candies each day and loaded up trays for the customers on all of the counters. The smell of her Christmas peppermint tea and sweets was rather overwhelming. I mentioned to them that it was late summer and not yet time for the holiday uproar. Elsie replied that she was of the opinion that my customers and myself would benefit by the holiday spirit whether it was actually the holiday or not. It seemed to me that she was right in that a little uptick in positivity might be appreciated by the future consumers, so I pretty much just sat and watched all of their cheeriness materialize into a rather delightful jewelry store.

The happiness of Anna and Elsie, and the increasing beauty of the surroundings also made my spirits lift a bit. It wasn't even terribly bothersome to me that they insisted on bringing that little dog Sugar along with them each day. Elsie said that they certainly could not leave her home alone because she would get lonely. *(Good grief!)*

Customers actually enjoyed the little creature and lifted her up and petted her and fed her chunks of their helpings of Anna's cookies. We all were amused by the hysterical response that the animal would display at each hour and half hour when all of the store clocks chimed. She appeared to believe that we were being attacked by some regularly ding-donging alien species.

All of the activity of Aunt Anna, Elsie and Sugar, along with all of their women friends that came to the store to visit them, kept my mind off of the activities of George Volger. Anna even organized a knitting group which met at the store to complete their knitted Christmas gifts. This actually became a fairly large event, with Elsie and Anna providing instruction for ladies who needed some help and ideas for patterns for the making of winter caps, scarves and mittens. Elsie even brought in some of Anna's extensive yarn stash to the store to sell to the ladies. When I asked Anna if this depletion of her yarn supply bothered her she said, "Heavens no, Fitch. This allows me the pleasure of shopping for new skeins of yarn and provides me with the money to buy them."

****

It has been clear over the past few years, that holding an auction is a good sales strategy and particularly before the Christmas season. I announced in mid November that I intended to sell my entire stock of diamonds, watches, cut glass, silver, clocks, ivory, and in fact every piece of merchandise in my store at auction. All I require of customers is a deposit to secure the purchase until Christmas. I also provided chairs for the ladies and souvenirs for all of the participants. People are inevitably interested in purchasing their holiday gifts at the lowest price possible and the advertised sale draws their focus and their funds to the jewelry store.

Things were proceeding as usual with the anticipated increase in customer traffic when I experienced a dreadful shock. My auctioneer was arrested on Saturday night for not having the proper licensing for conducting an auction. A scoundrel named Floyd Crow filed the charges and a hearing was set for Tuesday. I appeared before the court and assumed responsibility for the non-payment of the license. I told the judge that "I have conducted auctions in the past and have never had to purchase a license. I have always secured the mayor's permission before but this time I neglected to do so. It was not my intention to evade payment or license. I thought that as a license was not required in the past it would not be required now." I paid for the license with a check for $50.00. (The Muscatine Journal and News Tribune, November 22, 1920, pg 1, "AUCTIONEER IS ARRESTED; SWAN ASSUMES BLAME")

Then, a few weeks later, J.H. Walter filed a suit against Joel McGary, my auctioneer and myself alleging that he purchased a watch at my auction which was represented as being worth $10.00. When he took it to another jeweler (Gee, I wonder which jeweler he took it to) he was told it would retail at about $ 7.50. (The Muscatine Journal and News Tribune, December 31, 1920, pg 4, "FALSE PRETENSES CASES DISMISSED") He said that he tried to return it to the Swan store but both the auctioneer and I refused to refund his money. (The Muscatine Journal and News Tribune, December 31, 1920, pg 4, "FALSE PRETENSES CASES DISMISSED")

Once again I appeared in court and found that the evidence against us was not sufficient for conviction and the charge was dismissed. I then refunded Mr. Walter with his $7.50. As I exited I saw Mr. Walter on the courthouse lawn and asked him if he could refund my reputation to me just as I refunded his money to him.

And that is the whole point. There is now no way that my reputation can be resurrected. I have been officially and publicly dragged through the mud. Not only have my so-called 'misdeeds' been the subject of interest in the local newspaper, but the court house staff is beginning to consider me a 'regular'. For a man who has never been in legal trouble of any type, I am now an easily identified transgressor.

To say that the business in my store dropped after my newfound notoriety is to put it mildly. I was embarrassed and humiliated by the events; my staff was embarrassed and humiliated, as were Elsie, Aunt Anna and all of my customers. Nobody wants to go holiday shopping at the establishment of the 'newly degraded' for fear that they will come into actual contact with the disgraced. All of the holiday decorations on earth will not bring back the holiday spirit.

Although there is no concrete proof, I am perfectly aware that George Volger is behind all of these legal troubles. During this time Volger has been displaying alleged "fake" jewelry in his shop window which he claimed had been purchased at auction. The man is trying to destroy me. He has been taking pleasure in building his own fortune by demolishing mine. He will have a price to pay for this treachery some day.

Elsie

We women have been fighting for the right to vote for a very long time. It has been a difficult and emotion packed journey. I can recall hearing about the President of the United States actually being hissed by suffragist delegates in 1910. President Taft was welcoming the delegates to the convention of the National American Women's Suffrage association when he informed them that he was not altogether in sympathy with their cause. He said that he thought one of the dangers in granting suffrage to women was that women as a whole were not interested in voting and that the power of the ballot would be controlled by the less desirable class as far as women were concerned.

After the women in the crowd began hissing at his remarks, he said, "Now, my dear ladies, you must show yourself capable of suffrage by exercising that degree of restraint which is necessary in the conduct of government affairs and not by hissing. If I could be sure that women as a class would exercise the franchise I would be in favor of it. At present there exists in my mind considerable doubt. Permit me to say that the task before you in establishing our political rights is not in convincing men, but in convincing your own."

Mrs. Philip Snowden, a suffragette from England, while attending the local Chautauqua, indicated that this was primarily the fault of the husbands. In comparing our suffrage movement with that of England, she said that "If American women were not treated so well, they would have voted long ago. The majority of them are spoiled by the men so they do not ask justice for the minority. It is a curious survival of your colonial days, when women were scarce and held as treasures, your men have never gotten over that attitude." (The Muscatine Journal, August 3, 1910, pg 2, "GREAT ENGLISH SUFFRAGIST TELLS OF MOVEMENT IN BRITISH ISLES")

She identified three primary reasons that were given for denying the vote to womankind: "One being that women's place is in the home; another that women cannot fight and assume the physical responsibilities that men can; and that women don't want it." (The Muscatine Journal, August 3, 1910, pg 2, "GREAT ENGLISH SUFFRAGIST TELLS OF MOVEMENT IN BRITISH ISLES")

There continued to be an ongoing view that the majority of women were not interested in the affairs of government and in voting and that they would not go to the polls. In the elections at which women were allowed to vote in Iowa, it was a common observation that the ladies demonstrated a lack of fervor for the right. In fact, the day before the President's hissing incident, it was noted that few women voted at the vote on the question of issuing $40,000 in bonds for an addition to the high school, while the men thronged to the polls. (The Muscatine Journal, March 3, 1910, pg 4, "FEW WOMEN VOTE AT THE ELECTION")

Perhaps the most annoying rationale was presented by a man in my bible lesson class. He said that women should not be given the vote because they will only vote how their husbands tell them to vote and it will therefore essentially be giving 2 votes to the married men.

This passionate dispute continued throughout the years until our right to vote was ratified by the States in August ensuring that we will be able to vote in the national election to be held in November. Aunt Anna and I earnestly sought to prepare ourselves for the presidential contest of Warren G. Harding against James M. Cox.

We attempted to get an idea from Fitch of what to expect at the polls. We cornered him the evening before the election and obtained all of the information that we could about the process. He assured us that there would most probably be special instruction and special assistance provided for the ladies since this would be their first voting experience. We made arrangements to all go to the polls together, the first thing in the morning.

I awoke on election day at dawn and could already smell the pancakes. I donned my robe and slippers and danced down the stairs to find that Aunt Anna had already set my place at the table along with a cup of coffee. "What do you think we should wear today, Elsie? I have no idea of what is proper voting attire."

"I don't think there are any rules yet established, Aunt Anna. It seems appropriate to wear our 'going to church' clothing. Let's have a part in setting that as the voting day standard. I am going to don my very best hat with the feathers and carry my favorite tooled leather purse for the occasion."

"Then I will do exactly the same," replied Aunt Anna.

We returned to the kitchen after we were fully dressed and marveled at how stunning we both looked. Aunt Anna said, "I think we will be the most stylish voters at the polls."

"Now there is an important factor," replied Fitch.

"Don't be sarcastic, Fitch. We ladies have been struggling to experience this moment for about 70 years."

Fitch dropped us off at home after we voted and headed to the store. A steady stream of lady friends and neighbors visited to talk about the voting experience and to perform our very first voter analysis of what we expected as voting results. We learned a few days later that the total popular vote increased dramatically for this election from 18.5 million in 1916 to 26.8 million in this election.   (https://en.wikipedia.org/wiki/United_States_presidential_election,_1920) Warren G. Harding won by a landslide.

On the day of the election I was informed that Des Moines had instructed county clerks that women were to be added to the jury lists in all of the counties in the state. Women on juries means women making legal decisions in the courts. This cannot be true!

Just think about it: "In the early 1800's married women could not own property in their own right and could not make legal contracts on their own behalf. In most states, women could not even have custody of their own children. According to state laws, children 'belonged' to their husbands. It was not until the 1840's that the laws began to change and women could own property in their own right after marriage or obtain custody of their own children".(https://www.nwhm.org/online-exhibits/rightsforwomen/index.html)

Right after the election, Carrie Chapman Catt who had been a leader in the women's suffrage movement moved to convert it into the League of Women Voters.   (https://www.nwhm.org/online-exhibits/rightsforwomen/index.html)   I   am excited about this effort to assist women in being educated and informed voters in the future. Not only have women demonstrated that we want to and can vote in this election, but we now have the opportunity to demonstrate that we will also be knowledgeable and wise citizens.

In addition, prohibition was finally put into effect on a national basis in January, although Iowa has been dry for some time. While there have been rumors about racketeering and bootlegging in the area, they will never cause as much damage to families as the legal liquor business has. I can't help but to feel satisfaction over all of this. So many wonderful dreams have become reality for so many of us this year. It is a wonderful time to be alive.

****

Aunt Anna and I decided to reach out to assist Fitch in the store late in the summer. He continues to be experiencing a period of sadness and also has been complaining about a back ache. We thought that we could add some energy and laughter to his life so we stuffed Sugar in the automobile, along with a few dozen treats and boxes of ribbons, pine cone and fir branches and headed for the store, although it was actually only the end of summertime.

Fitch was surprised to see us but seemed to take pleasure in all of our efforts and even in the antics of Sugar. He was pleased to observe how positively the customers responded to her. It appeared that the word was getting out that you could visit with the entire Swan family plus the puppy when you visit the Swan store. The foot traffic increased significantly.

Then Aunt Anna got the idea that she would move her knitting circle to the store and there consequently ended up being throngs of women gathering to participate. As most women are aware, knitting and quilting circles are the center of news and information among us ladies. Fitch was not aware of the draw of such activities and this gave him a rare opportunity to experience the internal functioning of a female social circle.

He very much seemed to enjoy his time with the 'ladies' and was beginning to regain his appetite and to even smile and laugh periodically. I was feeling such relief up until the time that a series of charges were filed against him and his auctioneer. It was spread all over the newspapers and was the talk of the town. It broke my heart to see Fitch ready himself for court. I never thought that I would observe him in such a state of humiliation.

Aunt Anna had complete dinners prepared and steaming on the table for him when he arrived home after his court hearings. I am certain that she knew that it would be unlikely for him to have much of an appetite after such an experience, but she knew of no other way to express her emotions toward him. We would all sit around the table, attempting to force food into our mouths, while he informed us of the goings on.

The number of customers shopping in the store declined. Aunt Anna and I stopped visiting when the level of activity sank and we all found ourselves sitting and staring at the door, waiting for a customer to enter. "I think this is bad for my mental health," I said to Aunt Anna. "Let's go home and prepare it for the holidays."

We put a fir tree in the living room with a few candles and decorations. We lacked the energy for more strenuous activity. I spent my days sitting in the kitchen and watching Aunt Anna make an effort to bake a few sweets. It was clear that things were really going downhill when Aunt Anna had lost the baking fever.

****

Our spirits were raised when David would drop by for walks with Cookie and Sugar. There were many times when we would not leave the home at all but would sit in the parlor and bask in the warmth of the fire with cocoa. Aunt Anna and I felt our spirits lift when we were in David's presence and we began to spend our afternoons playing card games or telling stories while the dogs entertained themselves in the dining area.

David would try to remain after Fitch returned home to engage in conversation with him but Fitch did not seem to be at all interested. He was never rude to David. It is not in Fitch's behavior to be rude to anybody. However, he couldn't seem to keep up with it all. His eyes would lose focus and it was clear that his mind was in another world. David would usually end up saying, "I can see you are tired from slaving in that store all day, Fitch. I will go and let you catch up on your sleep." When Fitch would offer no response, David would put on his coat, pick up Cookie and leave quietly.

George

I was surprised and delighted this morning to learn that the Democratic Party had nominated me to be their candidate for city alderman from the second ward during their convention yesterday evening. I had not the slightest notion that I was under consideration for the position. Although humbled by this selection, I had to inform them that it is not possible for me to be a candidate for the office and that I cannot accept this honor. (The Muscatine Journal and News Tribune, February 12, 1920, pg 2, "CANDIDATES TO TRY ALDERMANIC RACE ARE NAMED")

I am so pleased to be chosen by these people. It is a concrete indication of the level of trust and confidence that the people in this community have of me. It is not possible for me to run for political office for a number of reasons: I really do not have the time to take away from my family and business responsibilities to give the position the attention that it would deserve. I also do not always agree with the Democrats about everything and they would be certain to discover that once I was in office. Although in the main, I am most certainly a Democrat, I do not want to be put in a position where I am expected to endorse every Democrat notion. At times the Republicans support the right policy as far as I am concerned.

In addition, it would hurt my business and rightly so. I could not blame my many Republican customers for not supporting my business interests, if they hear me espousing philosophies which are contrary to their own. That is just plain common sense.

Helen agreed with my decision. She has become very interested in politics now that she can vote at national level elections. The woman read everything that she could find about the presidential candidates, Warren G. Harding and James M. Cox. I believe that she knows more than any person on earth about the League of Nations which was the primary focus of the campaigns. As she searched all papers about that issue she also made note of every other candidate and every other issue. I could tell by my conversations with her that she could ascertain the nuances and analyze the complexity of the issues with much more clarity than I. There had been such a high level of concern expressed by some of the local men that wives would vote how their husbands told them to vote that she asked me as we left for the polls, "Well, George, aren't you going to ask me how I am going to vote?"

"No," I replied, "I am afraid that I will vote however you tell me to vote." We both laughed all the way to the polling place.

****

Over time, I have become quite annoyed about Fitch Swan's practice of holding a jewelry auction every December. It seems like he is attempting to lure customers away from me, not by expert craftsmanship, but by undercutting price and quality. I cannot afford to allow that to happen. The holiday business is too critical for my bottom line.

Although I do admire the man for his offensive tactics, it is very clear to me that he is ordering poorly made, cheap products to sell through his auctioneer at inflated prices. The customers believe that they are getting a good deal and cut prices on his regularly stocked items. They are not aware that they are being flooded with cheap junk that he would normally never stock on his shelves. I am sure that he is making good profits from this move but it really does not fall within the definition of responsible business practices, in my view.

I could not help but notice the crowd that this auction attracted. As usual, his auction this year is scheduled to occur right at the beginning of the holiday season to facilitate his need to suck the community dry of all excess spending money before the onset of Christmas shopping. Some of my regular customers were attracted to his auction by curiosity and ended up buying a few items. They came into my store afterward to show me their goods and to brag about the fact that the prices that they paid were well below any prices that I have listed for comparable items.

I got out my ordering catalogues and we searched through them to locate their auction purchases. They were shocked and, a few of them, quite mad at the inflated suggested retail prices that they had been quoted. Some of them were loaned to me for the purpose of creating a display. I exhibited in my show windows, samples of the fake jewelry, which have been forced upon auction patrons. (The Muscatine Journal and News Tribune, August 2, 1921, pg 5 "BITTER TRADE WAR ENDS IN DOUBLE TRAGEDY WHEN SWAN SLAYS VOLGER, ETC.")

Instead of developing a well thought out defensive strategy, Mr. Swan became so incensed by this act that he brought legal action for damages against me. (The Muscatine Journal and News Tribune, August 2, 1921, pg 5 "BITTER TRADE WAR ENDS IN DOUBLE TRAGEDY WHEN SWAN SLAYS VOLGER, ETC.") "Original notice of a $10,000 suit for damages was served upon me shortly before Christmas Day." The suit was never formally filed in court, however, I assume because Mr. Swan, upon investigation, probably discovered that the jewelry was indeed fake. It is amazing to me, how vulnerable a man can be when he reaches his seventies.

****

I surprised Helen with a bit of news on Christmas night. We sat before the fire after the usual holiday hubbub that occurs at our home. We always prefer to exchange our Christmas gifts on Christmas evening after the children are tucked happily in their beds and all Christmas visitors have left, food has been put away, dishes washed and dried. We sat contentedly and watched the embers spark and crackle. Helen gave me a wonderful throw that she had made for the store. She had carefully crafted it out of blocks of dark colored flannel and had embroidered pictures of all of my favorite river wildlife upon it. She said that she wanted to make certain that I was always adequately warm at the store and that she had picked out colors that would match with the store interior. It, of course was beautifully done. I don't think that there is anything that Helen cannot do.

She opened the envelope that I handed her and took out the little map that I had drawn. "What is this, George?" she asked.

"It is the proposed location of the branch store that I want to open in Davenport next year. We now have enough savings and are bringing in enough profits to make this addition. Davenport is one of the fastest growing cities in the state and it is sitting on the Mississippi right across from the city of Rock Island, Illinois. The total number of potential shoppers in that area is phenomenal. We stand to reap huge profits, Helen."

"Oh, George, I am so very glad to hear this and will help with this venture as much as I am able. Life is so exciting with you by my side, George. I always feel like we are embarking on new adventures. Maybe we will end up with enough stores to provide businesses for each one of our children to inherit. They will start their adult lives with a great advantage."

Chapter 11: 1921
Fitch

At this point in time I believe that the people of the community are not yet aware of the extent of my economic problems. Although I have experienced a long and gradual financial decline, I have done my best to keep this secret from my neighbors and family.

My jewelry business is essentially ruined. Very few customers visit the store. I have cut the hours for my employees and am doing most of the remaining work myself. When the staff asked if this was permanent and if they needed to be looking for other employment, I told them that it was an 'after the holiday season' decrease in staff hours in order to compensate for the common 'after the holiday season' decrease in purchases. They seemed satisfied with that explanation.

Yesterday I laid off the cleaning lady and now will need to clean my own store. For some reason I find this to be a most embarrassing occurrence. It has been a long time since I have had to mop up after myself. Perhaps I am fortunate that there is no foot traffic in the store to witness this humiliation.

****

I spend most of my days reading poetry that I have secretly written, over the years, into journals and have hidden in the corner of the safe. Nobody is aware that I have long been a writer of poems about the river. I have never revealed them because I believe that they are an expression of an inner self that I have not wanted the world to share. Others do not need to know of the depth of my feeling. It does not seem to be what the world defines as 'manly'.

I get one journal out at a time each day and hide it under papers at the counter so that it cannot be seen if a customer happens to wander in. I find myself reading them over and over and at times, I observe a tear fall down onto the page.

It is probably a good thing that alcohol is outlawed at this time because I fear that it would become my constant companion.

I often wonder if Elsie will continue to love me when she becomes aware of the depth of our economic difficulties. She is cognizant that there has been a decrease in business in the jewelry store. Anyone walking down Second Street who compared the throngs of people crowding into the Volger store with the cobwebs hanging in my doorway would be aware of that fact. When she asked me if everything was going alright, I told her that the store is in a bit of a downward spiral but that my investments are our major source of support. As far as she knows, profits in the store are irrelevant to our economic welfare. She is not aware that the investments have all collapsed.

She has assured me that everything will be fine and that we do not need to live in the level of luxury that we have in the past. We do not need to take the extravagant vacations that we have, nor do we need to support all of the organizations that have sought our donations. She thinks that if she stops buying the newest fashions the budget will be balanced and that if we eat less often at the fine restaurants all will be okay.

She does not understand what the economic loss will mean. It is not the loss of a vacation. It is the loss of a home. It is not a matter of shopping less. It is a matter of not owning a car to take her shopping or anywhere else. It is a matter of her not being able to have her hair done, or of needing to sell her jewelry. It is a matter of not being able to afford her long and costly visits with the Drs. Braunwarth. It is a matter of her neighbors no longer recognizing her and of all of the friends in her various women groups no longer acknowledging her existence. It is the matter of no longer being the wife of the most successful businessman in town and is instead a matter of being the wife of the biggest disgrace the community has ever known.

The community will pity and will laugh. They will laugh because I was not brought down by power and authority, strength or even wisdom. I have been disgraced by an arrogant young man. I assumed that people would not be fooled by this game player and that they would be disgusted by the lack of decency of his behavior and the injustice of the position in which I have been placed, but they are not. The fact that he was nominated by a political party to run as a city alderman attests to that fact. I have never been so nominated.

****

My beloved sister, Harriet, Mrs. Charles Cadle, passed away in her home in Muscatine.

She was my only living sibling. All of my biological family was now gone: my mother, father, sisters and brother. Only my nephew Cornelius remains. He will need a great deal of support after this loss and I am in no position to offer him sustenance of any kind.

I was unable to engage in much conversation with anybody during Harriet's funeral. My sorrow was so great that I found it difficult to get up and dress for the ceremony. Elsie had to help put on my clothing, shave and comb my hair. I sat next to Cornelius in a stupor during the funeral proceedings. Elsie held on to my arm and helped me stand up and sit down during the appropriate times.

Although Elsie had a reception after the burial, at our home, upon my arrival, I immediately went to bed upstairs. As I lay with my eyes closed, I heard a sound in the hall. Cornelius cracked the door and said "Uncle Fitch, are you awake?"

"Yes, Cornelius. Come on in. I share your sorrow at the loss of our beloved Harriet but I don't have the energy for a conversation right now. Perhaps if you come back tomorrow we can talk about old times."

He walked inside, closed the door behind him and sat in the over-stuffed chair at the end of the bed. "Thank you, Uncle Fitch. I have something I want for you to know. I had a visit with George yesterday. He stopped by the house to express his regrets to me about the loss of Mother. I hesitate to mention this to you, but I do not want to see you hurt any longer. I think we both have experienced enough sorrow. He said that people all over town are talking about Elsie. They have seen her about town with David Porter and there are questions about the extent of their relationship."

I lay silently for several minutes. A sudden rush of heat coursed through my body. I bolted upright and said "Would you please repeat that, Cornelius?" He repeated that George Volger had expressed concerns about Elsie's behavior in the community and her fidelity to me.

"I know David Porter quite well and Elsie and I both have a friendship with David and you can go back and tell George Volger to shut his mouth. I better never hear him spreading any rumors about Elsie again!"

"Settle down," replied Cornelius, "I figured that there was some kind of explanation. I am sure that Elsie is as loyal to you as you are to her. I just thought that you needed to be aware of what is being said in the community."

After Cornelius left, I was surprised to feel a tear flow down my cheek. "I

181

must not let myself wallow in sadness," I said to the empty room. Truth be told, none of this misery is because of me. This devastation had occurred because of the actions of George Volger.

George had caused the sky to fall down upon me. Life was fine until I met and tried to help that worthless piece of trash.

Although I have never had any children, I have had my Elsie, and I have had my reputation. I am about to lose everything for which I have ever worked. But the fact that tortures my soul beyond endurance is that I will soon lose the respect and regard of my community. The community would soon observe the esteemed community father, numbered among the men of affluence, renowned for my business acumen and stability, crumble. I simply cannot and will not face the humiliation.

I will never be able to deal with my problems if I succumb to self-pity. I must grasp the anger and remain strong so that I can stop this man. I will not let him win. I will show him who has the most power and the most strength, in the end. Anger feels so much better than the sadness of my losses. Anger forms a molten wall that blocks out the unendurable sorrow. I must hang onto the anger. I gave that ingrate training. I picked him up off the streets and taught him all that he knows. He owes everything he has to me. Rather than expressing gratitude, he has done everything in his power to destroy my life and he has been terribly successful at it. He will not benefit any longer by the fruits of my destruction. I will win in the end. I will put a stop to all of this.

****

June was a horrible month and July promises to be even worse. Because I will soon have insufficient funds to pay my bills, I have taken out a $10,000 mortgage on my home Sheltering Oaks. (The Muscatine Journal and News Tribune, August 2, 1921, pg 5 "BITTER TRADE WAR ENDS IN DOUBLE TRAGEDY WHEN SWAN SLAYS VOLGER, ETC.") It was my hope that this would sustain us for a while but money was draining out of my bank account like water running down a drain. This need to place Elsie's home in financial jeopardy angered me greatly. How could any person find pleasure in this sinister plot against Elsie and myself? The man is evil. I will not allow him to observe Elsie's losses. He will not feel pleasure in her pain.

On July 24th I transferred my Cadillac license into Elsie's name at the office of Fred Nesper, county treasurer. (The Muscatine Journal and News Tribune,

August 2, 1921, pg 5 "BITTER TRADE WAR ENDS IN DOUBLE TRAGEDY WHEN SWAN SLAYS VOLGER, ETC.") My goal, of course, is to keep the creditors from going after the car. It is unlikely, however, that she will be able to afford to keep it in the future.

When I arrived home on July 28th, Elsie surprised me with a party. It was my 71st birthday and she had gathered neighbors to celebrate that and the 45th anniversary of my jewelry business. To say the least, I was in no mood for a party. It was all I could do to keep from screaming at her, "Elsie, did you not hear my voice when I told you about our financial problems? Do you think a party is a good way to deal with such an issue?"

At the end of the evening she gave me a brand new hat as a present. It was a handsome fedora that she purchased at the haberdashery in Davenport. *I give up.*

I wore my hat to the store the following day because there seemed to be no possible way to benefit by not doing so. My banker came to speak with me but excused himself when Julius Hayden, a salesman from New York walked in and interrupted. I am certain that he did not feel comfortable discussing private banking matters in front of others.

Although I was frustrated by the departure of my banker, I approached the subject with Julius of possibly returning some of my product and getting my money back in exchange.

He said that he would look into the situation. *Of course he will. I trust that about as much as I trust my banker to find time in his busy day to deal with me.*

****

I am sitting in my store listening to the hollow ticking of the clocks. This store is feeling more and more like a prison. Not only am I in confinement, but I am in isolation in this prison. The solitude of this empty wooden box has its advantages. I no longer want people to enter this space. I have nothing to say to them. If I find the energy to arise and open the door and step outside, I might come into contact with somebody who expects me to converse, expects me to listen and expects me to care. Thus I cannot leave but must stay, and sit, and listen to the damn clocks tick.

I pick up the daily newspaper and glance at a headline on the front page. There, in big letters, is the announcement that George Volger plans to open a jewelry and optical store in Davenport in August. (The Muscatine Journal and

News Tribune, July 30, 1921, pg 10,"August 10 Opening Date for Volger Davenport Store") Plans have been finalized and a manager has been secured. He is quoted as thanking the citizens of Muscatine for their ongoing support which has caused his business to prosper and expand. He looks forward to a long and rewarding future both here and in Davenport.

I had to catch my breath. *Oh my God! Oh no. That will not happen. I will destroy this scheme of yours. I will finally, once and for all, stop your evil.* As a symbolic gesture of the demise of George's new business I decided to burn the paper. "I will put that damn thing up in flames," I said aloud.

I stormed through the back room, grabbed my matches and bent down to light the paper on fire on the back steps. As I looked up to make certain that there was nobody near to observe the behavior, I noticed Elsie and Sugar in the alley behind the Volger store. She and George were engaged in some type of conversation and I saw him reach out and touch her neck.

I hastily ducked back into the store. Dizziness overcame me and I sank slowly down against the safe. As I attempted to steady my breathing, my eyes focused on the 'Love is a Cottage' painted on its door.

I felt a spark of anger surge within me. *It is no longer my business and reputation in the community that this scoundrel is after. It is the one thing in my life that matters the most. It is my home, my cottage, my Elsie. It is the last straw. I will not allow him to hurt my Elsie. This will come to an end. This is over!*

Elsie

I am relieved that the Christmas season has passed. Aunt Anna and I did our best to help Fitch build a holiday atmosphere in his business which would attract customers. I think that our actions did make some difference but once the newspaper suggested to the community that we might be auctioning off poor quality goods, the bottom fell out.

Aunt Anna and I decided to switch our efforts to the home front and to create a happy holiday home instead. I would try anything to improve Fitch's attitude. He mopes around all of the time but instead of closing early, or taking weekends off, he is actually spending more hours sitting in that store. I have attempted to convince him that remaining in the store and spending hours brooding on the lack of customers does no good for the business and particularly does damage to himself. It seems that he has stopped listening. Nothing is moving past his exterior shell.

Things worsened dramatically with the death of his sister Harriet. I do not understand the impact that her loss had on him. I anticipated that his sadness would increase dramatically, but his mood switched from sadness to fury. Instead of being tired and withdrawn he became energetic and combative. The smallest things seemed to get on his nerves.

Fitch has always been a mild and gentle man and consequently has never learned to express anger productively. When he becomes enraged, he begins to breathe rapidly, his muscles tense and his face turns red but no expressions come out of his mouth. He looks like a balloon that is filling with air until it reaches the point of explosion. When it gets bad enough for him, he removes himself to the Indian mounds and becomes consumed by the vista of the river.

I do not think that this is helping him. I finally met with Dr. Sarah to get some ideas about dealing with this situation. It certainly helped my mood to open my heart and let all of my concern flood out. As is her common practice, she listened quietly but attentively.

After I had fully expressed my anxiety, she informed me that I was doing a very good job of attempting to deal with a very difficult situation. She explained that reaching the seventies is, at times, a difficult period in life for a man. He may sense the waning of vitality and strength that passing the seventies mark can signify. This worry will most likely lessen for him as time passes and he notices that most of our notions of aging are basically myths. We all age at our own rate according to a multitude of factors. There are no simple equations indicating that at sixty we will have these capacities and at seventy we will have these. She said that I need to make certain that I am continuing to give Fitch the message that I continue to appreciate him and support him.

Dr. Sarah gave me a prescription for a calming tonic which I was to have filled by her sister's pharmacy downstairs. She then told me, "Elsie, the most effective way of dealing with this situation would involve Fitch coming directly to me for counseling. Please attempt to convince him to do so."

"Thanks, Dr. Sarah," I replied.

As I left I reflected that there is no way in this world that Fitch is going to discuss his feelings with anybody. I cannot even get him to discuss them with me. On top of that, he is not going to speak about his feelings with a doctor. To say he would not view that as proper and manly is to put it mildly. Add to that the fact that Dr. Sarah is a woman and you have reached the realm of the impossible. Never in this lifetime will Fitch ever be seen entering the offices of female physicians. That is not going to happen.

****

Fitch's seventy-first birthday was just around the corner. I spent some time contemplating how I could best deal with this potentially harmful age marker. I came up with the brilliant idea of throwing him a surprise party to celebrate not only his birthday but also the anniversary of the founding of his business. This will serve to take some of the focus off of the aging of his body and move it to the successful establishment of a business tradition in this community. I only invited a few neighbors because Fitch does not seem to welcome a lot of social interaction at this time. When he arrived home he drifted through the evening like a ghost and as soon as was possible, retired to his bedroom.

The next day Aunt Anna commented that I sure seemed to put in a lot of effort to plan a surprise for Fitch that he seemed to not appreciate. She knew how difficult it was for me to get to Davenport to purchase that hat for him. My motivation was an ongoing concern about him possibly becoming ill by sitting in the park without an adequately warm head cover. His back has been hurting him and I worry that it may be a symptom of some growing illness.

I thought about Aunt Anna's words while I was in my dressing room, preparing for the day. As I stood before the mirror, I spoke to my reflection. "You know that Aunt Anna is right, Elsie. You seem to be becoming insignificant to Fitch. He hardly notices all of your efforts to make him happy and to provide him with a comfortable and welcoming home. You are getting lost in all of this. You really do have the right to occasionally hear a word of thanks. You are a person who lives here also. You deserve some affection and recognition yourself."

I searched through my jewelry box, as was my daily practice, to find the right decoration for the wife of the 'town's premier jeweler'. The Lake Superior agate that I found at the river's edge flashed as it caught the light.

I placed it around my neck and said to my reflection, "That is the perfect gem for you. Somehow it has become lost in the conflict between two men. All seemed to not recognize that it was you who found this beauty and it should have remained about you but instead became all about them. You have wanted to wear this for some time, want to wear it now and you will wear it now."

As we ate breakfast I noticed Fitch staring silently at the agate. "I know that you do not appreciate this necklace, Fitch, but I love it. The river left the stone for me and I had the good sense to appreciate its true beauty. It means a lot to me and has nothing to do with you." He did not reply but placed his coffee cup in its saucer, wiped his mouth with the napkin and left for work.

****

A lot of my time is being spent with Sugar in my lap. Petting her soft fur and receiving her many doggie kisses makes me happy again. It makes me experience love.

David and I continue to walk with Cookie and Sugar, but I often find myself roaming around town with Sugar in between our visits. I am taking her for more and more walks and find that, not only does she love exploring the community, but that all of the fresh air and exercise is doing me a lot of good.

I have heard the rumors about George's plans to open a branch store in Davenport and I am quite happy for him and Helen. His family has grown throughout the years and it will provide the extra funding that he needs to support them. It will also be wonderful if he could manage to have a business for each child to take over when he retires.

I do not think that this information has yet been shared with Fitch and I have no intention of doing so. He continues to view himself as being in a personal competition with George for worth and value. It is likely that he will not have a positive view of the planned expansion.

As I was walking Sugar down the alley that is behind the Swan and Volger stores, George came rushing out of the back door and almost ran right into me. He spent some time laughing at and playing with Sugar. "What a lively little thing," he said.

"She is my little sweetheart," I responded. "George, congratulations on your expansion into Davenport. I wish you the greatest success with the venture."

"Thank you, Elsie," he replied.

When his eyes focused on my agate necklace, he reached out and touched it and said, "You are still wearing that lovely stone, Elsie. It seems like you found it a lifetime ago. Time seems to move so rapidly. I hope things are going well for you and Fitch?"

"Actually things could be going a little better, George. Speaking of time, I think that Fitch is nearing the point of retirement. I am happy about it because he deserves to spend some time fishing and bird watching and generally having fun rather than working all of the time."

"How wonderful for Fitch," he commented. "He has earned a happy and active retirement. Send him my regards."

George

I have to be the luckiest man on earth. Helen began a ritual of having us list all of the things that we are thankful for as we sit to eat lunch after church each Sunday. She thinks that it is a good method to instill a positive and grateful attitude in our children. It has become a problem recently because we now have so many items to list that our children become restless and our meal cold. We agreed that we are not going to be able to keep this practice up for much longer.

The icing on my 'cake of life' is my children. George Junior has already been giving us glimpses of his intelligence and athleticism at the age of seven. He has begun his school years in a very positive fashion. His brother Charles was born after four years and Helen hurried to have Marion a year after. My home is always alive and active with the energy of these little children. I will do everything in my power to make certain that their lives are full of love and happiness.

Planning the expansion of my business into a neighboring community has been an interesting and productive process this spring. My plans are working like clockwork.

It looks as if everything will be in place to open in August. I was excited to learn that my friend and staff member, Newton Quinn was willing to take the position of active manager of the new establishment. His agreement is a great stress reliever for me because he is competent, friendly and honest. He will be the perfect manager.

I have also been negotiating with L.A. Willits who is presently an optometrist in Davenport. It is my hope to contract with him to provide services for the optical department that I plan to include as part of the new business venture. It appears that jewelers are increasing their involvement in the eye glass area. It promises to be economically successful for the future. Good vision is important in today's world and with the advances in the field of

189

optometry it is now possible to provide positive assistance to people with vision problems and frames can be designed to compliment every face.

****

One very sad event has occurred and it is the death of Harriet Cadle, Cornelius' mother. I think it was sudden and unanticipated by everyone. The moment that I heard that Cornelius had returned to the community from Des Moines and was in his family home, I drove over to offer him my condolences.

After he welcomed me inside, I gave him a big hug and he escorted me to the parlor. "I have brought something for you, George," he said. "Something to take the edge off of the sorrow." He reached inside of the credenza and pulled out a couple of bottles of beer.

"Where in the world did you get these?"

"Oh come on, George," he replied. "Beer is everywhere." He then reached inside the credenza and removed an entire gunny sack full of alcohol.

While we sat and sipped our beers, Cornelius filled me in on all that had been happening in his life since the last time we were together. He seemed to enjoy working in Des Moines and was not wanting to return to Muscatine permanently unless the death of his mother makes it necessary. He said that he did not plan to go back into business with his Uncle Fitch. Although he stated that he appreciated all that his uncle has done for him, he does not think his presence is advantageous to the store. He said, "How many times can I go into the jewelry business and fail before I come to the conclusion that I am not cut out for the business? I do not want to cause my uncle any more grief than I already have. In addition, I know how close he was to my mother and how devastated he is by this loss. I don't want to cause him any more suffering."

"I don't want to be rude, Cornelius, but I think your alcohol is killing me," I said. "Where did you get this and what in the world is it made out of?"

Cornelius laughed and responded, "I don't mean to brag but I have my very own bootlegger. God only knows what it is made out of. Could be gasoline, or turpentine or maybe even horse urine." At that he dissolved in spasms of laughter.

"I think I need to go home, Cornelius, while we both still have our wits somewhat about us. One thing I want to mention to you before I leave is that I have some concerns about your uncle's welfare also. I have been hearing many rumors about Elsie over the years. If you want to keep your uncle from getting

190

hurt, I think a little hint or two could serve him well. Elsie has been observed walking around the town with David Porter lately. I wonder if you might want to suggest to your Uncle Fitch that perhaps he needs to keep a closer eye on his wife. Helen tells me that my imagination is getting the best of me and that I should put no stock in gossip. I do not wish to add any additional stress to your situation but the funeral may give you a chance to talk to your Uncle Fitch. Meanwhile Helen also sends you her sympathies and hopes that you understand that she cannot free herself from the children to attend the funeral services."

****

When the heat of July arrived, my life was the busiest that it had ever been. In addition to all of the planning for my expansion, I had responsibilities to fulfill as a member of the board of directors of the Muscatine baseball club. A lot of effort was expended striving to help the club secure the very best athletes in the area to ensure their future success. I also attempted to find time every evening to play some catch with little George. It is not only fun, but it is my responsibility to start the training of his athletic skills at a young age. While the other children run and play in the back yard, he concentrates on doing the very best that he can. It will be just a few years before I will be watching him play ball with the Muscatine baseball club.

****

When I was working busily last Friday evening a traveling salesman, Julius Hayden came into the store. He mentioned that he had just visited with Mr. Swan. He said that when he arrived in the establishment Mr. Swan was engaged with another gentleman who he indicated was a Davenport banker. Just as Julius introduced himself, the banker left. This seemed to greatly agitate Mr. Swan who stated with a certain amount of anger, "I wanted to talk to that man badly. It means so much to me."

He then told Mr. Hayden that he was in serious financial straits. "Through the efforts of my friends, I have gotten into a lot of trouble," Mr. Swan said, "and I suppose they will get me into court soon and I will be in a lot of trouble."

The salesman reported that he then began a tirade against me and claimed that my competition had been very dirty and his (Swan's) business had suffered

191

heavily from it. Hayden said that Swan had been returning large amounts of products which he had ordered and on which he was unable to make payments. He told Mr. Hayden that "there is going to be a big surprise around here one of these days".

I admitted to the salesman that there were bitter feelings existing between the two of us. I informed him about Mr. Swan's holiday auction sales which impacted greatly on my own business. I assured him that Mr. Swan certainly was not the only merchant in town who suffered from competition. It is a management issue for all of us.

At the same time, I was shocked to learn of the depth of Mr. Swan's financial difficulties. I had no idea that he was in such a desperate position. It is unbelievable that he is blaming all of his difficulties on me. He cannot fix the issues within his own control if he cannot see them because of his focus on myself.

****

Helen expected me home early for supper Saturday evening but my conversation about Mr. Swan had broken my concentration. I was surprised to hear the clocks chimed on the hour, grabbed my coat, locked the back door and ran right into Elsie Swan and her little white dog.

She had heard about my business expansion and congratulated me on the new venture. She then mentioned that her husband was at the point in his life where he is seriously considering retirement.

I noticed that she was wearing the agate necklace that I crafted for her and was reminded of all of the years that have passed since I was a young clerk in the store of Mr. Swan. So much time, so many transactions, so many life changes have occurred since then.

I thought about all of the years of effort that Mr. Swan has put into his store and imagined how devastating the loss must be to him.

I have sufficient funds to expand my business and perhaps the bankers would also back me in the purchasing of the store from Fitch Swan. That would kill two birds with one stone: it would ease Swan's financial problems and it would also ensure my own spot as the premier jeweler and watchmaker in Muscatine.

I contemplated the possibilities all Friday night and the more I thought about the potential, the more excited I became. I mustered all of my courage and called Mr. Swan after I closed my store for the day on Saturday and informed him that I had a business proposition for him that involved purchasing his store and would like to meet him at my jewelry store on Sunday morning. I said that I hoped we could settle any misunderstanding and disagreements that exist between us. He agreed to meet with me the following morning.

****

I awoke early on July 31st. The sunrise flashed across my eyes as a gentle breeze blew the lace curtains at my bedroom window. Although the heat usually made it difficult to get a good night's sleep at the end of July in Iowa, I had slept like a baby. I smiled to myself as I mused that everything was falling into place. My plans and my business and my dreams for my family were finally coming to fruition.

I seemed to have been born under a lucky star. This day promises to be very rewarding. I had planned this morning to motor to Wilton to meet Gayle Lindeman who is the pitcher for the Muscatine baseball team. (The Muscatine Journal and News Tribune, August 2, 1921, pg 5 "BITTER TRADE WAR ENDS IN DOUBLE TRAGEDY WHEN SWAN SLAYS VOLGER, ETC.") I had hoped to pick up William Holliday around 8:00 am to drive to Wilton with me, but William was only able to accompany me if I postponed my trip until noon. I informed the pitcher that plans had changed and we would arrive closer to noon. This change allowed me to partake of a Turkish bath in the morning and meet with Mr. Swan before embarking on the baseball venture.

****

I could hear the clatter of dishes and silverware as Helen prepared the table for breakfast while the children made their usual Sunday morning sounds. I jumped out of bed, put on my robe, and joined my family for breakfast.

After outlining my morning plans for Helen, we talked about spending some family time together in the afternoon. So much had been happening lately, that it was difficult to find the time for my wife and children that I desire. I asked her if she would contact my two brothers and two sisters who also live in town and invite them to come over for an afternoon get together. I will be able to make all of the necessary family contacts in one afternoon.

I want to make certain that they are thoroughly informed about the latest details of the expansion. Dr. Willets, the optometrist and myself have reached an agreement and he will be available to provide the optical services. Although the jewelry store in Davenport is scheduled to open on Wednesday, August 10th, my new manager Newton has already moved to Davenport with his family over a week ago and is now supervising the installation of the store fixtures and cabinets. We plan to open the doors early Wednesday to work the kinks out of the system and to have the actual formal grand opening on Saturday, August 13th.

It is possible that some of my extended family members would like to share in the organizing of the grand event. I think they might enjoy participating in all of the excitement. I will talk with them about it this afternoon after my meeting with Fitch Swan.

****

When I was at the Muscatine Hotel to partake of the Turkish baths, I put the upcoming meeting with Fitch Swan out of my mind. I could practically feel my body absorb the vitamins and minerals while I soaked in the warmth of the steam. The men and I chatted about the prospects of the baseball team and the pitcher that I plan to interview in the afternoon. I did keep one eye on the clock. Jewelers and watchmakers often were very prompt and I didn't want lateness to cause a bad start to my meeting with Mr. Swan.

Book 2

Come join me at my water's edge
beneath the molten foam
and cradle in my ancient soul
to find this place called home.

Fitch Swan awoke to the familiar resonant tick-tock-tick-tock of the grandfather clock. It was one of the most skillfully carved and crafted clocks that he had ever purchased to sell in his jewelry store. He was certain that he could have made a large profit on its sale but Elsie had taken a particular liking to it. He had been awakened by it each morning since he moved it up to their second floor bedroom as a surprise gift on the night of their wedding, fourteen years ago.

Fitch's sleep had been fitful, restless and unsatisfying during the night. Part of it was due to the insufferable oppression of July heat in Iowa. Even though there were large open windows on all sides of his bedroom and a turret in which wind could blow from nearly every direction, it was really too hot and humid for sleep.

As he arose, he put on his robe and stepped onto the small second story balcony. He reflected, *The only thing more hot and unbearable than an Iowa July, is an Iowa August.* There was some pleasure in the notion that he would not be here to experience another heat wave.

I do not deserve any of this. I have struggled to make something out of my life. I have worked long and hard for my business and for this community. I am one of the people who make a difference in this world. I am not only a respected businessman but I am also a jeweler, an artist whose media is gems, stones and precious metals. An artist... a businessman ... a community leader.

195

I will never have to feel anything more than I have today. I will not spend any more time in the hell that my store has become. I will not feel any more sadness and anger than I have already felt. I refuse to experience any more humiliation and shame. Tomorrow will not be better than today or than my yesterdays. There is no reason to hope. There is no reason to go on.

Fitch observed the rise of the sun over Weed Park accompanied with the usual chatter of squirrels and bird songs echoing up and down the hills and valleys. He felt his eyes begin to tear as he reflected on the fact that the years he had spent as park commissioner may be the only positive benefit of his lifetime of efforts.

He engaged in his ritualistic morning preparations. Although it was a very hot Sunday, he dressed in the usual jeweler's three-piece suit and stiffly starched white shirt. He placed his best gold cufflinks into his cuffs and a stickpin in the knot of his tie. He shaved his face, trimmed up his mustache and combed the closely cropped gray hair. *Neat and tidy,* he thought. *It is important for a jeweler to be neat and tidy.* Cleanliness allowed the beauty in life to shine forth and cleanliness had always had importance to Fitch. As he glanced at his reflection in the mirror, it occurred to him that nobody would be able to guess what he had in mind. His face showed no sign that he had it all planned out like clockwork.

The odor of bacon, eggs and coffee emanated from the kitchen as he descended the staircase. Elsie had the fine china set out on the dining room table in preparation for his Sunday breakfast.

"How are you this morning, Fitch?" asked Elsie. "You were tossing and turning all night. Maybe we should consider traveling to a cooler climate in the summer next year. We could go north. I understand there are many pleasant places around the lakes in Wisconsin and Minnesota."

"We'll see, dear. I just need to eat my breakfast and get downtown. I really don't want to think about anything else right now." Fitch sat down and began eating his breakfast.

"It is something we need to think about in the future," Elsie replied. "Perhaps we can talk about it this afternoon. I will invite the Hunts over and we can ask them about their cabin on Lake Superior in Minnesota. They seem to so enjoy spending their summers in that location that they are now there much of the year.

"Excuse me, Fitch but I have to go upstairs and get ready for church. I had trouble sleeping in this heat too so I am running a little late. I want to get there

196

before everyone is seated so that I get a good seat. It is important to be close enough to the minister to see his expressions when he talks, and to be as far as possible from the crying infants at the back. I guess I will see you this afternoon."

This was their normal Sunday morning routine. Fitch had been so long in the habit of working in his jewelry store on Sundays that Elsie had given up attempting to convince him to attend Sunday services. She, on the other hand, was a devoted member of the Baptist church and considered its members to be like family to her. She prided herself upon rarely missing a service.

Fitch was surprised to find that he enjoyed the meal; in fact he finished all of the bacon from the platter and put an extra dollop of fresh creamery butter on his bread. It had always been his habit to watch his food consumption very carefully. It had taken all of his will to pass up Aunt Anna's cookies, pies and cakes.

He recalled the sweet corn that was so present in Muscatine at this time of the year. It drove him crazy. His standard July dream was of sweet corn, ice cream and fudge sauce and the Midwest's famous potato salad. He could hardly even stand to think about fried catfish fished straight from the Mississippi. The food of the Midwest is one of life's local pleasures that he had denied himself. He had always had such extraordinary self discipline. It surprised him to find that food seemed to be the last pleasure he had in life. It was probably because he felt the freedom from the need to worry about weight. No need to try to look young and fit. No need to continue to appeal to Elsie.

****

Oaks shaded the walk as he headed toward his garage and climbed into the freshly washed and polished car. He loved this car. As he climbed into the driver's seat the smell of warm leather filled the interior. Fitch backed out of his garage, rolled down the driver's window and met the scent of lilac that grew so profusely in his neighborhood.

He felt that this car accurately reflected his success and standing in the community. It was the proper automobile for a man who lived in this house, on this street, in this neighborhood. It was difficult to accept that he no longer owned his precious vehicle. *I will not allow myself to think of that,* he thought. *I must keep away from the pain. It is too deep. It reaches into my soul now. I will shut it off. I will turn off my heart and my mind. I will now just follow the plan.*

197

He pushed the starter button and the engine sputtered to life with a rumble. How much the world seemed just like every other day. The sky was blue, the grass in the lawns all the way downtown were green verging on overheated brown. He noticed how the leaves in the trees were curled upward towards the heavens searching in vain, for any drop of rain… reaching up to the heavens for sustenance. He had given up on that notion a long time ago.

He had tried prayer 19 years ago when Mollie Howe Swan became ill. She had been such a believer. She would attend the Baptist church even when she did not feel well. Her prayer vigils never ceased until her demise in 1902. Fitch felt that if prayer did not work for as holy a woman as Mollie, there was no way it was going to work for him. Mollie had been such a loss to him. In fact, when Elsie initiated the pipe organ fund for the Baptist church, Fitch supplied the memorial organ as a gift in memory of Mollie. (History of Muscatine County, Iowa, Irving B. Richman, Supervising Editor. Chicago: S. J. Clarke Publishing Co., 1911. 2 v., pg 89)

Oh, Mollie, Mollie. How different things might be today if you had just survived. Our generation understood the meaning of loyalty. The young people today do not. I hope you understand what I must do, Mollie. There have just been too many losses here. I want to come and join you.

Fitch arrived at 122 East Second Street and pulled into his parking space at the back of the jewelry shop. All was quiet on the outside of his store. He took a moment to stand on the stoop and watch a gull fly over the Mississippi. He thought he could hear the far off rumble of a train on the tracks that ran along the river. He was mistaken. He rather liked the way that the engineers sounded their horns when they entered the downtown area. It made him think of far away places, of unknown people, of life that existed just beyond the horizon. It promised future adventures, waiting possibilities, coiled strands of hope waiting to spring forth.

No. It was best that there is silence this morning. Silence keeps one in the here and now. Silence makes us open our eyes to what is before us. It glues us to today and all that we need to deal with and endure. It quiets the music of our hopes and the melodies of our memories. *It focuses me on the now and on the plan that I have decided that I must now carry out.*

Fitch entered the door and walked into the back room. He opened the window and breathed in some fresh air and noticed that there was nobody in the alleyway at this time of the day on a Sunday. The curtains fluttered from the open windows of the upstairs apartment above his establishment. He could hear the shrill whistle of a tea pot coming from the upstairs kitchen where a lady lived in an apartment. Fitch always appreciated the fact that she was quiet and particularly that she minded her own business and did not try to befriend him or bother him while he was in his store. She never bought jewelry or came in for the holiday entertainment. She seemed to not even realize that he existed here, below her.

Oh well, she probably couldn't afford jewelry, he thought. *Most of the people who live above the stores in the downtown have more immediate uses for their money. What is the use of going into a jewelry store if you can't afford to buy anything? It would just make a person feel humbled and embarrassed. She probably is a very nice lady. She most certainly had enough taste to rent an apartment that was a block from the river. From her windows she could watch the sun rise on the Mississippi. That certainly reflects her worth.*

There were several guns in his store. *A jeweler needed such things for protection. After all, a jeweler's wares were worth a lot of money.* He silently opened the drawer beneath the mahogany cut glass cabinet near the front room and considered both of the revolvers that rested inside. He passed over the larger caliber revolver and picked up the 32.

The 32 was loaded and ready. Fitch placed it carefully under the counter while he watched out of the front plate glass window. There was nothing to do now but wait. He felt remarkably calm as he observed the street, waited for the designated time to arrive and listened to the soothing tick-tock-tick-tock of the jewelry store clocks. He knew George would be on time. Jewelers and watchmakers were painstakingly precise.

****

So he thinks he is going to open a branch store in Davenport and become a known quantity in southeastern Iowa. He is like a snake that will swallow my store and then slither forth, spreading his influence beyond this community. He thinks that, within time he can consume anything that he desires. A big ball star... a big ladies' man... big businessman.

I, on the other hand, will sink into oblivion. He will watch as my business closes, he will expand into my space and I will lose all of the respect and positive regard of the community. I will be embarrassed and humiliated. Elsie and I will lose our home and I will probably lose my Elsie, who is the only important part of my life that remains intact.

199

Then I must consider this all from how it will impact Elsie. He thinks he will watch as she loses her home and all of her possessions. He will observe her while she is shunned by her ladies' social groups. He will see her when she loses her love for me and becomes hopeless and vulnerable.

****

The din of the clocks in the Swan store all striking the hour at the same time, startled Fitch out of his reverie. He found it difficult to catch his breath. He picked up his hat, opened the door and walked down the street just in time to see George Volger arriving from the opposite direction.

As they met they shook hands, and laughed a little about meeting at precisely the correct time. Fitch suggested that they move to his store so that George might have an opportunity to assess the value of the inventory. "William Kindler told the police officer that he saw Mr. Swan meet Mr. Volger at the front of the store and that the two walked to Mr. Swan's store talking and laughing as they went. (The Muscatine Journal and News Tribune, August 1, 1921, pg 5. "Bitter Trade War Ends In Double Tragedy When Swan Slays Volger, Etc.")

George hadn't been in the Swan store for many years and he was pleased to get an opportunity to see what treasures it held. Mr. Swan had a pretty good reputation for attention to detail. Perhaps the shop would need no remodeling at all. They engaged in small talk about the quirky nature of the diamond industry, the health of their families and the heat of the day, as they proceeded down Second Street to the Swan store.

Fitch unlocked the door and stood aside as George entered first. George said, "Everything looks like it did when I first began working here." He worked his way through the jewelry boxes and cabinets. He checked through all drawers and cupboards. He took the gems out of their cases and held them up to the light coming through the window. "I could have never imagined that I would own this store one day. Even though I am opening a big store in Davenport in a couple of weeks, I believe I have the resources to take this over also. I'm glad that I am in a position to help you out."

With a smile frozen on his face, Fitch said, "Let's go to the workroom in the back where we can talk about details while we sit down." Fitch followed George toward the back of the store. As he passed the counter, he picked up the 32.

When George saw the 'Love is a cottage' safe he reached out and touched its smooth surface with his hand. "I had forgotten all about this. I remember how much Elsie loved it. I want this to be included in the sale so that I can use it and preserve it in this room. Elsie, and you also for that matter, can come to visit it at any time that you would like."

Fitch replied, "Don't talk about Elsie, George. I wish you had not been spreading lies about my Elsie. She was never anything but nice and kind to you and you need to treat her with kindness in return."

Without turning around, George said, "Well, Fitch, I am not certain what you are talking about but if you look at this the right way you would see that what I am doing is a major favor to Elsie. Because I am bailing you out of trouble, you might have enough resources left to support her. It would break my heart to see Elsie lose her home. I know that all that you and Elsie have is the house. What I am doing is saving you and Elsie of course, from the public humiliation of losing everything that you own."

Fitch quietly raised his hand and pulled the trigger without a word. He watched the bullet hit the back of George's head, enter just a little bit and explode. As millions of tiny specks of blood, brain, hair and gunpowder showered the room, George fell face first onto the floor with a loud thud. Fitch listened to the harsh death rattles of George's breath for several minutes until all fell silent. He watched with fascination as blood sprayed on the 'Love is a Cottage' on the door of the safe and pooled under George's head.

****

"Miss Sarah Bilkey lived in the flat over the Swan jewelry store. She was preparing her tea when she heard a booming sound come from the store downstairs. She assumed that Mr. Swan had dropped some heavy object or closed the cellar door in the rear of the building. She listened more carefully throughout the remainder of the morning but only heard the indistinguishable muted rumble of voices from below and Mr. Swan passing in and out of the store. She said that she did not hear any voices raised above a natural conversational tone." (The Muscatine Journal and News Tribune, August 1, 1921, pg 5. "Bitter Trade War Ends In Double Tragedy When Swan Slays Volger, Etc.")

****

Time now moved very slowly for Fitch. It seemed as though he was a person existing outside of himself again, calmly watching that man known as

Fitch move forward with his plan. He picked up a cloth that he used for polishing jewelry and wiped the gun clean. He opened the mahogany cabinet with the cut glass and placed the gun back in its proper place. He must keep all about him neat and tidy. He wiped the blood spatters off of his hands and suit, locked his store and walked to the "Western Union office to send a telegram to his wife's sister, Mrs. Milan P. Harlow of Hartford, Connecticut. The message was filed about 11:00 am and said, "Come at once". (The Muscatine Journal and News Tribune, August 1, 1921, pg 1. "CITY SHOCKED, GEORGE VOLGER SLAIN BY F.W. SWAN; LATER THEN KILLS SELF; ACT PLANNED.")

****

Elsie returned home from church shortly before 11:00 and was immediately struck by the quiet and emptiness of her home. She went searching for Aunt Anna around the house but determined that she must be participating in the social gathering after the Zion church service. She picked Sugar up and put her on her lap, and rocked her on the front porch while watching the families gathering for picnics in the park across the street.

Gosh, I feel lonely suddenly, she thought. "Sugar, you just are not enough company for me right now. I think I need a companion who can actually talk with me for a while."

She attempted to phone Fitch at the store to tell him that she wanted him to come home early for dinner. The operator who answered informed her that the line to the store was out of order.

****

Swan returned to his store, unlocked the door and entered the front room. He tore two pieces of paper off of the notepad by the telephone on the counter. He picked up his favorite pen and wrote, "I have killed George Volger. His body is in the back of the store." He placed his store key with that note and put it in his vest pocket.

Fitch then felt anger flow back into his body, from the tip of his pen and onto the paper of the second note. He wrote of why he had murdered George Volger. "He wrote bitterly of George and his years of 'dirty competition'. He described the mountains of anguish that George Volger had caused him. But, above it all, he said that he could not stand for the other man 'lying' about

202

those who were near and dear to him and that he would 'stop his vile tongue'."
(The Muscatine Journal and News Tribune, August 1, 1921, pg 1. "CITY SHOCKED,
GEORGE VOLGER SLAIN BY F.W. SWAN; LATER THEN KILLS SELF; ACT
PLANNED.") Fitch folded and sealed the note and addressed it to Chief of
Police Bronner.

Fitch put this note in his pocket along with some potassium cyanide crystals
that he kept in a jar for jewelry cleaning. He locked his door as he left the shop.
"He was observed on the street leaving the store by William Kelly, who was
standing on the corner of Sycamore and Second Streets. At 11:40am Paul
Steinmetz talked to Mr. Swan on the street. He said that the jeweler appeared to
be undisturbed and not excited in the least." (The Muscatine Journal and News
Tribune, August 1, 1921, pg 1. "CITY SHOCKED, GEORGE VOLGER SLAIN BY
F.W. SWAN; LATER THEN KILLS SELF; ACT PLANNED.")

Fitch felt nothing now. He was empty. He simply had to continue to move
forward to complete all of the steps of his plan, to tidy it all up. He entered the
Rankin funeral parlor and lay down on the sofa in the front room. The tick tock
of the clock in the corner was the only sound that reached him. He
methodically took the notes out of his pocket and placed them on his chest
along with the key to his store and removed some potassium cyanide crystals
out of his pocket. As the clock ticked towards its deep and melodious song of
noon, Fitch swallowed the crystals, and waited silently. Soon the ticking
stopped.

Epilogue

The exact contents of the sealed letter that Fitch Swan wrote for Chief of Police Bronner were never disclosed. It was reported at the time, however, "that the Swan letter wrote bitterly of Mr. Volger using such extravagant language as to fortify the theory that his long time grudge against the latter had grown until it had affected his mind. In the letter, it is understood, Swan declared that he did not mind Volger's 'dirty competition', but that he could not stand for the other man 'lying' about those who were near and dear to him, and that he would 'stop his vile tongue'."

The funeral of George H. Volger took place on Tuesday, August 2nd, 1921 in his home and at the Masonic Temple. Attendance of the service at the family home, which was restricted to neighbors, family and close friends, was conducted by the Reverend C.L. Young, Secretary of the Muscatine Y.M.C.A. and former pastor of the United Brethren Church. After the service Mr. Volger's remains, accompanied by the Knight Templars in full uniform, were escorted to the Masonic Temple where Masonic rites were conducted. Hundreds of Masons, members of civic groups, friends and acquaintances attended the service at the Temple. Places of business, as requested by the Association of Commerce, the Rotary club and the Lions club, closed for a half of an hour, during the burial, as a sign of respect for Mr. Volger. His burial took place at Muscatine's Greenwood Cemetery. He was exhumed and buried in Muscatine's St. Mary's Cemetery shortly thereafter. Helen Volger died in 1954 and was buried in St. Mary's Cemetery.

The funeral service of Fitch Swan was conducted in his residence by the Reverend E. M. Vittum, Pastor of the First Congregational Church, on Wednesday, August 3rd, 1921.

Mr. Swan was buried in the local Greenwood Cemetery with his wife Mollie on his left and their child who died at birth, to Mollie's left.

Elsie Swan inherited what little was left of the Fitch Swan estate. She remained in Muscatine for 5 years before moving to Waterloo, Iowa, with her Aunt Anna. In Waterloo, she obtained employment as a clerk and continued participation in her various women's groups to whom she gave presentations on the 'psychology of abundance' and 'the power of prayer in our lives'. In 1933, she gave a presentation to the Waterloo Roberson Club at the Y.W.C.A. on 'start afresh, the success journey'. She was a member of the Open Bible Church. Elsie died at the age of 65 of diabetic complications. She is buried at Greenwood Cemetery, on Fitch's right side in an unmarked grave.

On November 29, 1933, a notation in the Waterloo Daily Courier indicated that the application for the blind pension of Anna Fraleigh was referred to the finance committee. She was eighty-eight years old at the time. At the end of her life she was buried in Waterloo, Iowa.

Cornelius Cadle remained in Des Moines as an Edison phonograph salesman. He married and moved back to Muscatine in 1926. He died in 1927 and is buried at Greenwood Cemetery, a few feet away from the Swan plots, in a section including his mother Harriet and other Cadle family members.

The only heirs listed in Fitch Swan's will were Elsie and Cornelius. George was survived by his wife, Helen and his children George, Thelma, Charles and Jean. His children lived successful lives with one of his sons owning the Muscatine radio station for many years.

After Swan's death, the jewelry store was purchased by H. J. Theil of Chicago. It is interesting to note that $35.00 was received from the sale of the 'Love is a Cottage' safe.

Bibliography

1885 Iowa Census, Muscatine County

Bender, Alex, <u>Muscatine Fire Department : 128 years of dedication</u>, Muscatine, IA : s.l. 2003

http://collguides.lib.uiowa.edu/IWA0863, "Guide to the Sarah Braunwarth papers" cited July 2012

http://history1900s.about.com/cs/worldwari/p/lusitania.htm, "Sinking of the Lusitania" cited August 2015

http://www.dsaiowa.com/History.htm, "The Prohibition Years"cited August 2015

https://en.wikipedia.org/wiki/,"United_States_presidential_election,_1920" cited August 2015

https://en.wikipedia.org/wiki/First_World_War, "World War I" cited August 2015

https://www.nwhm.org/online-exhibits/rightsforwomen/index.html cited August 2015

Muscatine City Directory, January 1,1907, pg 66

Muscatine City Directory, January 1,1908, pg 352

Muscatine Daily Journal, November 6, 1883, pg 2, "Swan's New Safe."

Muscatine Journal, May 30, 1907, p4, Society Note, "Well Known Couple United in Marriage."

Oelwein Daily Register, January 15, 1916, pg 1, "MUSCATINE HAS FIRE SATURDAY"

Ostrem, Paul D.,<u>Dennoch</u>, Muscatine, Iowa , 2002."

Ostrem, Reverend Paul, http://www.elca.org/JLE/Articles697, "Loyalty Days"

Richman, Irving B.,<u>History of Muscatine County, Iowa, from the earliest settlements to the present time</u>;, VOLUME II, ILLUSTRATED,1911,THE S. J. CLARKE PUBLISHING CO., CHICAGO

Rousmaniere,Kate, Annals of Iowa,Volume 46, Issue 4 (spring 1982), "The Muscatine Button Workers"

The Muscatine Journal, February 5, 1901, pg 1, "Shots Fired at Mrs. Nation"

The Muscatine Journal, February 8,1901, pg 1, "Muscatine Saloon Keepers In Fear of Mrs. Nation"

The Muscatine Journal, February 9, 1901, pg 7, "More About Mrs. Nation"

The Muscatine Journal, February 11, 1901, pg 1, "Far Famed Smasher Is In Muscatine"

The Muscatine Journal, February 12, 1901, pg 4,"Company Breaks Up"

The Muscatine Journal, December 16, 1909, pg 45,"Muscatine the little dry town on the bend"

The Muscatine Journal, August 3, 1910, pg 2, "GREAT ENGLISH SUFFRAGIST TELLS OF MOVEMENT IN BRITISH ISLES"

The Muscatine Journal, February 23, 1910, pg 4, "F W Swan buys two lots in Fair Oaks"

The Muscatine Journal, March 3, 1910, pg 4, "FEW WOMEN VOTE AT THE ELECTION"

The Muscatine Journal, May 5, 1910, pg 1, "TRADE EXCURSIONISTS OFF ON BIG BOOSTER TRIP"

The Muscatine Journal, October 28, 1910, pg 5, "BUTTON WORKERS FORMING A UNION"

The Muscatine Journal, January 25, 1911, pg 7, "PLACE TIMEPIECE IN COUNCIL ROOM"

The Muscatine Journal, April 11, 1911, pg 4, Advertisement

"The Muscatine Journal, April 14, 1911, pg 2, "ANGRY CROWD THREATENS IMPORTED SPECIAL POLICE"

The Muscatine Journal, April 27,1911, pg 5, "DR. BATTEN TELLS OF BUTTON STRIKE"

The Muscatine Journal, May 11, 1911, pg 4, "Muscatine Young Man in Business"

The Muscatine Journal, August 31, 1911, pg 2, "CONDEMN CARROLL IN RESOLUTIONS"

The Muscatine Journal, October 19, 1911, pg 10, "ALERTS MEET AT THE CLUBHOUSE"

The Muscatine Journal, October 27, 1911, pg 2, "Police Clash With Crowds Near MKee & Bliven Button Plant"

The Muscatine Journal, December 19, 1911, pg 6, Swan Advertisement

The Muscatine Journal, December 19, 1911, pg 6, Volger Advertisement

The Muscatine Journal, February 5, 1912, pg 8, Cadle Store Ad

The Muscatine Journal, November 1, 1912, pg 5, "The Family In Revel at Sheltering Oaks Thursday"

The Muscatine Journal, May 6, 1913, pg 9, "GEO. H. VOLGER BUYS NEW JEWELRY STORE"

The Muscatine Journal, May 15, 1913, pg 5, Volger Ad

The Muscatine Journal, May 16, 1913, pg 10, "OPENING OF NEW STORE AUSPICIOUS EVENT"

The Muscatine Journal, May 17,1913, pg 5, Advertisement

The Muscatine Journal, November 5, 1913, pg 4, "Sanitary Drinking Fountain Arrives"

The Muscatine Journal, December 5, 1913, pg 12, "VOLGERS HOLDING AN ELABORATE OPENING"

The Muscatine Journal, January 17, 1914, pg 2, "PLANNED TO ORGANIZE NEW LOCAL BANK SOON"

The Muscatine Journal, April 13, 1914, pg 7, "LARGE CLOCK BEING INSTALLED AT PARK"

The Muscatine Journal, April 16, 1914, pg 9, "A New Boy Jeweler Arrives On Scene"

The Muscatine Journal, May 26, 1914, pg 2, "TO CONSTRUCT STEPS AT WEED PARK SOON"

The Muscatine Journal, April 9, 1915, pg 4, "VISITORS OF PROMINENCE AT THE HOTEL INAUGURAL"

The Muscatine Journal, April 9, 1915, pg 19, "7 BIG ICE BOXES WITHOUT ANY ICE"

The Muscatine Journal, April 9, 1915, pg 32, Advertisement

The Muscatine Journal, May 23, 2015, pg 1, "New business in Muscatine off to a running start"

The Muscatine Journal, May 24, 1915, pg 4, "Pioneer Jeweler to Retire From Trade"

The Muscatine Journal, May 26, 1915, pg 6, Swan Advertisement

The Muscatine Journal, August 14, 1915, pg 5, "Announce Revised List of Eligibles"

The Muscatine Journal, January 15, 1916, pg 8, "ICE HARVEST STARTS IN MUSCATINE TODAY"

The Muscatine Journal, January 15, 1916, pg 1, "Fire Destroys Store"

The Muscatine Journal, January 15, 1916, pg 5, "Fire Destroys Store"

The Muscatine Journal, December 14, 1916, pg 7, Advertisement

The Muscatine Journal, March 1, 1917, pg 1, "CONGRESS IS STIRRED TO ACTION BY GERMAN PLOT"

The Muscatine Journal, March 3, 1917, pg 1, BERLIN ADMITS WAR PLOT

The Muscatine Journal, April 13, 1917, pg 3, "FORTY YEARS AGO"

The Muscatine Journal, July 10, 1917, pg 4, "In Police Court"

The Muscatine Journal, September 20, 1917, pg 10, "WATCH STOLEN SATURDAY NIGHT"

The Muscatine Journal, July 12, 1918, pg 7, "Hold Farmer in Auto Accident"

The Muscatine Journal and News Tribune, February 12, 1920, pg 2, "CANDIDATES TO TRY ALDERMANIC RACE ARE NAMED"

The Muscatine Journal and News Tribune, November 22, 1920, pg 1, "AUCTIONEER IS ARRESTED; SWAN ASSUMES BLAME"

The Muscatine Journal and News Tribune, December 31, 1920, pg 4, "FALSE PRETENSES CASES DISMISSED"

The Muscatine Journal and News Tribune, July 30, 1921, pg 10, August 10 "Opening Date for Volger Davenport Store"

The Muscatine Journal and News Tribune, August 1, 1921, pg 1. "CITY SHOCKED, GEORGE VOLGER SLAIN BY F.W. SWAN; LATER THEN KILLS SELF; ACT PLANNED."

The Muscatine Journal and News Tribune, August 2, 1921, p 5 "BITTER TRADE WAR ENDS IN DOUBLE TRAGEDY WHEN SWAN SLAYS VOLGER, ETC."

The Toledo Medical Compendium, Toledo, Ohio, October 1891

www.usaiowa.com/images/Prohibition.pdf. cited July 2015.

About the Authors

Sharon and Tom Savage live in Muscatine, Iowa. They are prior owners of a bookstore on 2nd Street that was located between the historic Swan and Volger stores. Sharon has an MSW from the University of Iowa and teaches Abnormal Psychology and Sociology at the Community College level. She has been a social worker and a mental health therapist and has worked as a stringer for the local newspaper.

Tom has an MA from the University of Iowa, has taught Psychology at the Community College level, has worked as a college counselor, and teaches court ordered substance abuse, divorce management and family violence prevention classes. He is author of "A Dictionary of Iowa Place Names" and is an owner of an Iowa century farm.

CPSIA information can be obtained
at www.ICGtesting.com
Printed in the USA
BVHW081915230321
603224BV00001B/108